ABOUT THE AU

George G. Gilma
was then a small
attended local sch   ge of fifteen.
Upon leaving scho   abandoned all earlier
ambitions and decided to become a
professional writer, with strong leanings
towards the mystery novel. He wrote short
stories and books during evenings, lunch
hours, at weekends, and on the time of
various employers while he worked for an
international newsagency, a film company, a
weekly book-trade magazine and the Royal
Air Force.

His first short (love) story was published
when he was sixteen and the first (mystery)
novel ten years later. He has been a full-time
writer since 1970, writing mostly Westerns
which have been translated into a dozen
languages and have sold in excess of 16
million copies. He is married and lives on the
Dorset coast, which is as far west as he
intends to move right now.

The Desperadoes

George G. Gilman

NEW ENGLISH LIBRARY
Hodder and Stoughton

for
A.S.
California, here
we come – maybe!

A New English Library
Original Publication 1988

Copyright © 1988 by
George G. Gilman
First published in
Great Britain in 1988
by New English
Library Paperbacks

British Library C.I.P.

Gilman, George G.
The desperadoes.—(Edge; 58).
Rn: Terry Harknett
I. Title II. Series
823'.914   PR6058.686/

ISBN 0-450-42409-X

Printed and bound in Great
Britain for Hodder and Stoughton
Paperbacks, a division of Hodder
and Stoughton Ltd., Mill Road,
Dunton Green, Sevenoaks, Kent
TN13 2YA, (Editorial Office: 47
Bedford Square, London, WC1B
3DP) by Richard Clay,
Bungay, Suffolk.

1

The striking looking woman seated on the high-backed chair
behind the counter that divided the room into two unequal
sections was called Donna Terry. This was announced in
white lettering on a triangular-shaped block of wood, stained
dark brown, that sat on the counter top beside where she was
writing in a ledger.

Where she worked was at the Munro branch of the
Western States Bank, which comprised two rooms in a small,
one-story granite building on the north side of the
community's main street.

Munro was a fine looking little town in the Rocky
Mountains of Colorado's south west corner, close to the New
Mexico Territorial border.

Donna Terry was a neatly attired, attractive woman who
sparked a disconcerting sexual stir in Edge.

When he rode into town, the half-breed gave it only casual
attention: decided right off Munro was in most respects like a
hundred other towns he had passed through during his years
as a lone drifter. And since it was mid-afternoon and he had
no need to halt this early to supply the demands of hunger or
sleep for himself or his roan gelding, he expected to keep
riding on through: unconcerned by the mistrustful looks cast
toward him by the local citizens.

Then, threequarters of the way along the main thorough-
fare, Lark Street, closer to the western than the eastern limits
of town, he saw ahead on his right the familiar wooden
sign—its white-painted message confined to the left half of a
cut-out map of the US—of the Western States Bank. Which
caused him to angle away from the centre of the less than
bustling street, rein in his horse at the rail out front of the
bank.

He had been aware of a lessening of the tension—never dangerously high—as he rode by the midway point on the length of the street, kept his mount moving at the same even pace. Was seen to be a stranger with apparently no intention of calling a halt in Munro: unless, disinterested in all other aspects of town, he elected to stop by the Centennial Saloon to lay the trail dust in his throat. Which would have been no cause for immediate concern.

The majority of Munro's citizens were doubtless decent, quiet-living, law-abiding people, judging by the appearance of their town. The kind who would not welcome the disreputable saddletramp this stranger seemed to be. But if he did feel the need to stop over for awhile, best he rest up in the Centennial.

The saloon, with five horses standing contentedly at its hitching rail, was next to the bank, across a wagon-wide alley. So it was not until Edge swung down from his saddle, wound the gelding's reins around the rail out front of the bank, that most of those who watched him realised which of the two neighbouring buildings had caused the stranger to pause in Munro.

And without doubt, Edge pondered fleetingly as he crossed the sidewalk and stepped through the open doorway of the bank, he became the subject of rasping exchanges: as the quiet-living, law-abiding people of Munro voiced anxieties about this travel-stained, foreign-looking, mean-eyed, hard-mouthed stranger who entered the local bank.

A revolver butt jutting from the holster tied down to his right thigh.

Thus did Edge judge the effect he created on the community at large. But because he was so accustomed to being regarded with disquiet by people on first impression, he paid little attention to the almost tangible pressure of watching eyes he left out in the chill, sun-bright fall air. And welcomed the pleasant stove heat of the bank's interior: even more the warm smile of Donna Terry.

It was a habitual expression of friendly welcome as she looked up from writing in the bulky ledger on the polished counter top, and she obviously expected to see the familiar

8

figure of a regular customer she would know.

When she saw a complete stranger the amiable expression immediately faltered and the warmth in her eyes was displaced by fluttery nervousness. But she recovered from the jolt immediately: her mouthline had remained unchanged and it was a smooth, fast and easy process to resume the smile. Edge touched the brim of his hat, cracked a smile of his own that she did not see failed to touch his eyes as he said:

'Afternoon, ma'am. I guess this is the same Western States Bank has a branch in Cheyenne, Territory of Wyoming?'

'Why yes, I . . .' She needed to swallow that portion of her nervousness which created a lump in her throat. Then she blinked her big round blue eyes, completed: '. . . certainly think so. In fact, I'm sure there's a branch in Cheyenne. But I can check on that in just a moment.'

She reached to the side, slid open a drawer beneath the counter top, took out a sheet of paper, studied it.

Edge advanced across the thirty feet square public area of the room. Halted at a halfway point to remove his Stetson, grimly aware in the clean and recently repainted room of the trail dust dislodged from its brim and dented crown. But he spent only a moment with this inconsequential thought, then discovered a more obtrusive brand of self-consciousness bothered him: he was experiencing a totally unbidden stirring of lust for Donna Terry.

She was still a year or so the right side of forty, with the kind of figure—at least the upper half of it he could see above the counter top—that many women half her age might envy. Slender without any hint of skinniness, the curves of her body full enough in the right proportions to arouse the sexuality of any red-blooded man. Especially one who had been on the trail for many weeks while he kept his mind clear of unwelcome notions: probably the least pressing of which were concerned with women.

He had been in brief contact with over a score of women since he left San Cristobel in far off southern Arizona Territory. In trailside towns, at stage line way stations or on isolated ranches and farmsteads. And a handful of those he had exchanged the time of day with might have triggered the kind of emotion he felt as he looked at Donna Terry: but they had not.

Now, for no obvious reason, this blue-eyed blonde with the maturely pretty rather than beautiful face, an upper body demurely clothed in a high-necked, long-sleeved, crisply-pressed white blouse, had that effect on him. And next caused within him another feeling he at first failed to identify. Then realised, when she replaced the paper, closed the drawer, nodded and made an affirmative sound, that this was a sense of shame.

Which was damn fool crazy.

'Yes, sir,' she confirmed, nodded again to further express satisfaction at being proved right. 'There is indeed a branch of Western States in Cheyenne. Mr Abraham Nicholas is in charge up there.'

Edge was not embarrassed by the instant arousal he felt at first sight of this woman who was again easily smiling. Instead, it was because everything about her acted to underscore the sordidness of the events, far off in time and distance, that led him to stop off here today at the Munro branch of the bank.

'Is that all you require to know, sir?' she asked.

Her smile became less bright, but not because of nervousness. Instead, Edge thought, because Donna Terry realised what kind of interest she had unwittingly triggered in the man: and was disconcerted by her own response to the knowledge of this.

'No, ma'am,' he told her. Advanced across the rest of the public section of the room, placed his hat on the counter top in front of her name block, reached into the right hip pocket of his pants. 'I owe somebody in Cheyenne a hundred and fifty dollars. Planned to ride up there and pay it back in person. But I guess if I deposited the money here, the same amount can be paid to who it's owed in Cheyenne?'

She took a second too long to answer and it was plain this was not because she needed to think of a reply. She just was not fully listening to him as she came to terms with what she was seeing—and feeling.

She saw a man something over ten years older than her: a

10

big man, at least two inches taller than six feet, who weighed a solidly packed two hundred and some pounds. With Mexican blood in his veins: this seen in the Latin bone structure of his lean face and the skin tone a shade of brown established by heritage long before the burnishing effects of the elements had added their coloration.

The shoulder-length hair, too, although it was streaked with grey, was mostly of the kind of jet black that suggested Latin stock. And the man emphasised the Mexican set of his face by wearing an underplayed moustache which curved low at either side of his mouthline. This was just discernible in the middle of the afternoon, many hours since his last shave.

In contrast to the Latin look, his eyes were a glittering ice blue, the deeply crinkled skin around them suggesting they were permanently narrowed under the hooded lids. Also, the thin-lipped mouth, which held a smile line like it was an expression unfamiliar to the man, was as Aryan as his eyes.

So the stranger had mixed racial parentage and the resultant melding of features he had drawn from this could either be attractive or repulsive to women: their reactions to him dependent upon how they viewed the underlying latent cruelty that lurked within him.

He was dressed for the chill of a Colorado fall day in a short sheepskin coat that had seen much hard wear. His hat, the holster hung from his gunbelt and the pants and spurless riding boots, had seen long usage too.

But she saw it was not shortage of money that prevented him buying the outfit he badly needed when he produced a sheaf of bills from his hip pocket. He had much more than the hundred and fifty dollars he had mentioned.

'Yes, sir, you can certainly leave it to Western States to take care of that for you,' she assured him at length. 'You've no doubt seen we have a telegraph office in town. So we can wire Mr Nicholas at the Cheyenne branch. And the business can be completed by this time tomorrow, most probably.'

Edge finished counting off the money in fives and tens, said: 'I'm much obliged.'

Donna Terry said quickly as he made to replace the balance of the money in his pocket: 'There'll be a fee of three

11

dollars for doing the business, sir.'

He nodded, added three ones to the pile of bills he had been about to hand to her. And her smile brightened again for she was a professional at her business who had completed a transaction successfully. Just maybe her good mood was intensified by the fact this customer was such an unlikely looking one: who had frightened her, then attracted, even excited her.

When she took his money, she rose from the chair and turned. And he could see she wore a tightly fitted blue skirt that reached to midway down her high button boots. Then as she moved toward a large safe in the corner he saw that her lower body and legs were a match for her slender, alluringly curved torso.

She walked with easy grace, a natural sway to her hips: or that was what Edge guessed because, working in a bank, he thought she was not likely to be the kind of woman— certainly during business hours—to flaunt her feminine charms. Either with purposefully daring clothes or exaggerated movements of her body.

'I'll just see this is locked securely away, sir,' she told him without looking around from the green-painted, iron safe, six feet high by four feet square. 'Then I'll take a note of the necessary details I need from you.'

'Details, ma'am?'

'Your name——'

'It's Edge.'

She started to unlock the safe, which required both the keys she carried on a ring hung from the left side of the belt of her skirt.

'Right, Mr Edge. Also the name of the gentleman in Cheyenne to whom Mr Nicholas is to pay the one hundred and fifty dollars.'

He felt a fool again and vented a low grunt of annoyance with himself. Obviously she needed such details.

When she swung open the heavy door of the big safe four shelves could be seen inside: stacked with paper money, fabric bags of coins, heaps of documents and some ledgers similar in size and colour to the one she was working on when

12

he entered the bank.

'It's a lady,' he corrected. Experienced a mild feeling of disloyalty toward a woman who had been good to him in a time of need when he added: 'Using the word loosely, I guess.'

'I'm sorry?'

'Nancy Raven is a loose woman.'

Donna Terry glanced sharply over her shoulder at him, her eyebrows arched: but in an unrancorous mocking manner rather than shock. A smile continued to curve up the corners of her mouth.

Edge explained: 'Mr Nicholas at the Cheyenne branch of the bank will need to contact her at the Heaven's Gate Hotel, ma'am.'

'Miss Raven is a...?'

Footfalls shuffled on the roofed sidewalk which the bank shared with a row of stores on the other side from the saloon. And her expression as she looked toward the open doorway implied she hoped regular customers were not about to interrupt the talk she suddenly found as intriguing as the stranger himself.

'Right, ma'am,' he replied with a wry smile as she held back from voicing the word. 'That's what Nancy is. I'm not going to claim she's one of those with a heart of gold, but I've come across a lot more respectable women I don't think would have loaned me money on such short acquaintanceship. You have those details? Cash is for Miss Nancy Raven and her crib's at Heaven's——'

'Well, the man's talkin' of heaven and lookee here, good buddies!'

Edge had curtailed what he was saying an instant before the man with the croaky voice spoke: reacted to the way Donna Terry suddenly fixed her gaze on the doorway. Looked like she was seeing something a whole lot more frightening than her first glimpse of the last man to come into the bank.

'Hot damn, Ruben! Paradise is a ready open safe sure enough!' This one cackled liked he'd just told a favourite dirty joke, suddenly ended the sound when a third man snarled:

'Shut up, you sorry old fool!'

A fourth ordered, even-toned: 'Step away from that safe,

young lady. And leave it open the way it is.'

Ruben told Edge: 'And you reach for the roof, young feller.'

He had a Colt .45 rock-steady in his right hand thrust forward from his hip, trained on Edge's chest. In his other hand was a black, polished wooden cane which he brought up off the floor, waved high in the air for a moment to illustrate the order he gave.

Edge lifted his arms to the sides, bent at the elbows, until his splayed hands were level with the shoulders. Then drawled to the line of four men with aimed guns and kerchief masks concealing their lower faces: 'Okay, I've got the idea. It's a stick up.'

2

They were all elderly: this was plain from the crinkled flesh and watery eyes visible above the masks. It was also seen in the gnarled condition of their hands gripping the revolvers, and the way they moved as they advanced, shoulder to shoulder, across the bank: none of them painfully arthritic, but all with the stiffened joints and measured pace of advanced years.

But with the passing of these years had come experience. And it was clear they were well practised at holding guns on people while they robbed them.

'I don't believe this,' Donna Terry gasped, her tone incredulous to match the sense of what she said. 'I just don't belive this can be happening here.'

The man with the croaking voice, who wore wire-framed spectacles with highly magnified lenses, told her: 'Maybe not, but I reckon you're a young lady believes in God, though, Miss Terry. You don't move away from the safe like Pete told you, you'll pretty soon find out if there's any truth in that kinda belief.'

'Gene ain't the kindly old coot he sounds sometimes, lady,' Pete warned. He was afflicted by a twitch that affected the left side of his torso and his left cheek. But it did not impair the steadiness of his aim with the Colt in his right hand. 'He'll put a bullet right plumb between those cute little titties of yours easy as he'd swat a fly was botherin' him.'

Ruben moved in on the half-breed's right, slid the Frontier Colt out of the holster while Pete and the man with a stiff left leg trained their revolvers on him. And the bespectacled Gene continued to aim his Colt at Donna Terry.

Edge shot a glance at the woman and realised she had hardly moved since the four masked men appeared on the threshold. Except to become rigid: like she was on the verge of launching into some reckless move. He told her evenly: 'It's only money, ma'am. If you die, that's only good for paying the undertaker.'

She wrenched her gaze away from Gene, who was at the far end of the counter from the safe, lifting a flap in the top and pushing open a hinged front section. Now stared at Edge, at first with a puzzled frown, then a grim scowl. Seemed about to blurt out a stream of abuse that would place him in the same category as the four masked old-timers holding up the bank.

But suddenly the spirit drained out of her. She stepped back from the safe, raised her hands in the same manner as Edge, was abruptly sullen. Which seemed somehow to add a wanton quality to her look. But perhaps this impression was created because she was in an attitude of reluctant surrender, and the way her raised arms acted to lift and thrust the conical swells of her breasts.

'Wise lady,' Ruben complimented. Moved away from Edge and pushed the half-breed's Frontier Colt into his gunbelt behind the buckle, his own revolver back into the holster.

'Want you to know somethin', Miss Terry,' Gene said as he went past her and holstered his weapon. He reached the safe, swung the door open wider than she had left it. 'I would've shot you easy as Pete said. But I wouldn't have liked to have done it.'

'Quit the talk and make with the action, Gene,' the man with a stiff left leg urged.

'Yeah, hurry it up in there, you guys!' a fifth member of the gang rasped from out on the sidewalk. He sounded as old as those inside.

Gene had already begun to ransack the safe while he spoke to Donna Terry, continued to work at the same measured, efficient pace against the calls for haste. Shifted the bags of coins from the safe to the counter top. Then took out the stacks of bills, pushed them into a gunnysack he removed from inside his coat.

Edge watched this for just a few seconds. Tried to ignore

the angry-eyed gaze of the woman that constantly flicked around all the men in turn: viewed him with the same degree of animosity as the others. Then he looked at Pete and the stiff legged man, who kept their attention trained on him: further proof these men were no first-timers at the stealing business. They did the chores assigned to them at the planning stage, willing to wait until the proper time to look on the ill-gotten gains Gene took out of the safe, apportioned between himself and Ruben.

'Who you think you're lookin' at, mister?' Pete demanded sourly. 'You see him lookin' at us that way, Rich?'

'A hard man is all,' Rich countered. 'Who don't take kindly to a bunch of oldsters like us gettin' the drop on him, I'd say. Ain't that right, mister?'

'Hurry it up in there, Goddamnit!' the man outside urged.

'Just you take it easy or you'll wet your pants, Duff!' Ruben countered. 'Be through in a second.'

'You're right, I don't take kindly to what's happening,' Edge replied to the question from the man with a twitch. 'Particularly I don't like having guns aimed at me. You let it be known to the whole gang, uh?'

'Goddamn hard man!' Rich said.

Edge pressed on: 'You let it be known if any of you fellers points a gun at me again, he better be ready to kill me. Because I'll certainly do my best to kill him.'

Gene had emptied the safe of money, started to move back along the length of the counter. His gun was drawn again, his left hand clutching the bags of coins. Which left Ruben with the sack of bills. This was lighter and he could manage it with the same hand as the stick he needed to walk with. With the other hand he drew his Colt.

Gene growled: 'You want we should kill you now, mister? Save keepin' us all in suspense until the next time?'

Donna Terry made a deep sound in her throat that could have meant many things.

Edge had to look at her face to discover she was expressing a brand of contempt as her big eyes roved the room: again classed him with the bunch of old-timers robbing the Western States Bank.

Duff called anxiously from outside: 'Some folks are headed this way, you guys!'

'Let's get out of here!' Ruben ordered. As earlier, his tone of authority and the manner in which the rest of them responded branded him the top hand of the bunch.

Because of his need to use the stick, Ruben could not easily back toward the door. Likewise, the stiff-legged Rich had to face the way he went and shot anxious glances over his shoulder as Gene and Pete backed away, Colts levelled at Edge, eyes above their kerchief masks showing hard-set determination to do whatever was needed to carry through the bank robbery.

From along the street to the east, a man yelled: 'Hey, you people! What's up at the bank?'

'Hot damn!' Duff gasped in a strangled tone. And either he, Ruben or Rich fired a shot.

Gene and Rich both wrenched their heads around to peer out through the doorway as a discordant chorus of shouting sounded in the wake of the report.

Edge ordered: 'Down on the floor!'

He vaulted the counter. Had a blurred image of the woman as she switched her wide-eyed gaze between him and the doorway, shock and fear at last on her face. He also had a hazy impression of Gene and Rich snapping their heads around, aiming their guns again.

He hit the floor hard in back of the counter. As another gunshot exploded. Within the bank this time, and the bullet thudded into the wall. Closer to Donna Terry than to him, but not close enough to scare her into ducking behind the cover of the counter.

Edge felt a burning rage at her stupidity as he scrambled clumsily on hands and knees toward the woman, a cacophony of shouts and gunshots ringing in his ears: none of the raucous noise within the bank now.

'Down, you crazy bitch!' he rasped softly when he reached her, looked up at her as she stared down at him. Shock had turned to horror, and the horror held her more rigid than had shock. When she snapped open her mouth the look on her face suggested she intended to vent a tirade of scornful abuse

18

at him. But nothing emerged, until a man cursed and there was another shot inside the bank: this bullet came close enough to Donna Terry to trigger a scream from her. Which was suddenly more shrill when Edge curled an arm around the backs of her knees, rose high enough to thrust a shoulder into her thighs. And she toppled backwards, hit the floor with a force that shook loose a shriek of pain.

But then she folded up and tried to kick at him with both trapped legs, beat on him with tightly clenched fists. While she snarled incoherently in a way that suggested she intended profanities she could not call to mind even in such high anger.

For several seconds, Edge held on to the fighting, squirming, shrieking woman, only vaguely aware of the body of sound from outside the bank: shooting and shouting, the snorting of horses, then fast hoofbeats on hard-packed dirt.

Donna Terry, by accident or design, switched from a punching attack to scratching at Edge with clawed hands: and her long nails proved more effective weapons than fists. He felt sharp pain, warm blood running on a cheek, had a sudden very real fear of the woman gouging out an eye and released his double-arm hold around her legs.

Then she was immediately silent and he was certain there were just the two of them in the bank. He pushed himself on to his knees, hooked his hands over the counter top, levered himself up. Checked with his eyes on what his ears had indicated. Saw there was no one in sight. Not inside the bank, nor on those sections of the street visible through the open doorway and flanking windows.

'You keep a gun here in the bank?' he rasped at the woman.

Her breathing was laboured. Her staring eyes directed tacit hate up at him as she continued to sit on the floor.

He scowled and grunted. A log in the stove cracked and so did a bone in his ankle when he once more vaulted the counter. But he had made it just threequarters of the way to the open doorway when Donna Terry ordered calmly:

'Stop right there, Edge!'

He halted. Turned just his head, saw she was seated on the high-backed chair again: used the open ledger as a rest for the wrists of both hands wrapped around the butt of a cocked

Colt revolver. The gun was far from new but looked to be still serviceable. He could smell it had been recently oiled.

'Ma'am, I——' he started.

'I heard that braggart's claim concerning guns you made to your friends, mister! Now I have a warning of my own for you: move just one muscle and you'll have a hole in your back where you're not supposed to have one.'

A burst of gunfire momentarily drowned the beat of galloping hooves. Out along the western section of Lark Street. When it was over, Edge said against distant shouting:

'I was going to say, you've got me all wrong.'

She shook her head just once, hardened her expression. 'No, on the contrary, mister. It seems to me I have you dead to rights. And if I have to shoot you dead to stop you escaping, I'll be quite within my rights.'

A footfall sounded on the sidewalk and a man with a squeaky voice exclaimed: 'Oh, my goodness! Whatever are you doin', Donna?'

Edge shifted his eyes along their slitted sockets, saw a short, red-faced man wearing a white storekeeper's apron standing nervously on the threshold, Adam's apple jumping, button eyes blinking. He growled evenly:

'Making a point about the rights of women.'

3

There was an abrupt end to the noise out on the street. Except for the rapidly diminishing sound of pounding hooves on the open trail to the west of Munro. Then a voice was raised to proclaim triumphantly:

'Least we got one of 'em!'

Closer to the bank, a woman demanded anxiously: 'What d'you see, Vaughan? Is Miss Terry all right?'

The red-faced little man looked to the side, nodded and peered back into the bank. Then grinned, looked at his questioner again, nodded more emphatically. 'Yeah, she's well, Mrs Harvey. She's even captured another of the bank robbers.'

Edge let the tension of latent anger drain out of him. Had to suppress an impulse to a different brand of ill-humour when he wiped the back of a hand over his pained cheek, saw the smear of blood on it. This as he turned sideways-on to both the doorway and the centre of the counter where Donna Terry sat, the old revolver aimed steadily at him. A Navy Colt, he saw as he briefly studied the gun before he concentrated his attention on the grimly frowning face of the woman who held it.

'What?' she asked with a start. And there was a slight crack in her voice, a tiny movement at one side of her mouth to suggest the degree of strain she had kept hidden since she reached the chair, took the revolver from a drawer beneath the counter top.

'I didn't say anything,' Edge answered against a babble of talk and shuffling footfalls as people converged on the bank from both directions.

'Well, you looked as if you were about to!' she snapped. Moderated her tone before she went on: 'But I think you're perfectly right to save your breath and do your talking to Mr

21

Grimes when he gets here. See if you can convince the sheriff you didn't have a hand in the bank being robbed. You certainly won't be able to persuade me of any such thing, I can tell you that!'

Her voice was starting to crack again. It was obvious the woman felt the need to talk, to keep her mind free of notions that might raise doubts. Not doubts, Edge was sure, about him being a member of the bank robbing gang. Instead, of whether she could keep a grip on her self control; the gun aimed at Edge; her ability to squeeze the trigger should he make a move that forced such an action by her.

Then she was saved from further struggle to keep talking, prevent her voice from shaking as she searched for the words.

For another pair of booted feet rapped on the sidewalk boarding as the man named Vaughan backed hurriedly off the threshold. So a much younger, taller and broader man could take his place. A square-faced man with shiny black eyes, a slightly twisted mouthline and the kind of pale complexion that invariably accompanied his kind of auburn hair. A six foot, two hundred pound man of thirty years who, Edge thought, was not so confident as he tried to look. A man with a silver badge pinned to the upper left pocket of his vest, a Remington revolver levelled from his hip.

'All right, Donna,' he said, in a voice that was harder in tone than his face looked as he darted his eyes over the interior of the bank: kept the gun levelled unwaveringly at Edge. 'You can put the revolver down now. I have him covered. And you, mister, you get your hands up high above your head.'

His eyes were suddenly hard, like polished ebony, and his mouth was more twisted by the grimace. As the half-breed did as he was instructed, he decided it was the wan complexion that created a first impression of weakness in the lawman.

The body of subdued sound from outside seemed to emphasise the silence within the bank until the woman opened both hands so the gun slid free and lay on its side on the open ledger. Then she sighed, said with unashamed relief:

'Am I glad to see you, Mr Grimes. I just don't know how

22

long I could have kept up...' Abruptly she glared at Edge, hardened her tone to correct the false impression she might be giving him: 'But I don't tell lies, mister! If I'd needed to, I'd have shot you dead, make no mistake about that!'

Edge remained impassive.

The lawman told her placatingly: 'Don't you fret over it, Donna. You did just fine. Old Sam Parker, he winged one of the others. Two out of six right off isn't so bad. I'll get the pair of them locked up, then raise a posse, go round up the other four. Move out of here, whatever your name is!'

He gestured with his gun and stepped aside to leave the doorway clear.

'My hat?' Edge asked of Donna Terry.

She picked it up off the counter top with a grimace of disgust, scaled it across the room. Edge was able to catch it without moving his feet. Grimes watched him put it on, then snapped:

'I told you to raise your hands, mister.'

Edge did so and started towards the door as Donna Terry supplied:

'He said his name is Edge, Mr Grimes. Pretended he wanted to remit some cash to a woman of ... to a woman in Cheyenne. And the moment I opened the safe to place the money inside, his partners in crime rushed in and——'

'Details like that ain't too important right now, Donna,' Grimes broke in as Edge stepped across the threshold and coldly surveyed the street scene outside, read the hostility, revulsion and unease in many of the eyes that peered back at him. 'I'll get to them soon as we've——'

'You do whatever you have to so the whole bunch of them thievin' varmints are caught real soon, Harry Grimes!' a woman insisted: and bustled into the doorway as Edge reached the front of the sidewalk.

She was about sixty, grey haired, six feet tall, broad of hip and full of bosom. While this bulky form, dressed in dungarees, work boots, a man's shirt and a battered plainsman's hat filled the doorway between Edge's back and the muzzle of Grimes' revolver, there were stretched seconds when she provided a solid shield between captive and captor.

23

And more shouts rang out as Grimes and some of the people suddenly backing away on the street yelled at the woman, angry or afraid.

Edge thought there was maybe just time enough to get to where his horse was hitched, to slide the rifle from the boot, get the drop on one of the score or more local citizens out front of the bank.

But, he decided, the situation was not critical enough to merit the inherent risk: that if he did try to escape using a hostage, it was possible one of the Munro men might be tempted into making a reckless counter-move.

Then the brief period of high tension, which Edge alone seemed not to experience, was gone. The big, grey haired woman who he thought he heard named as Clara Cornwall, was inside the bank, cooing comforting words to Donna Terry. And was either impervious to, or chose to ignore, the insults snarled at her by Grimes.

When he saw Edge was still apparently as acquiescent as he had been since he was trapped in the bank, the sheriff suppressed his rage. And his manner was as coldly officious toward the townspeople as to Edge when he commanded:

'Clear a way for me and the prisoner, you folks! Excitement's over for awhile.' He stabbed a finger of his free hand toward a tall, thin man with a bald head and a squint. 'George, consider yourself deputised! Round up the other regulars! All of you be ready to leave soon as the prisoners are locked away.'

Many of those gathered out front of the bank had scurried several yards away when they recognised the danger after Clara Cornwall inserted her fleshy body between Edge and Grimes. Those who were left in a group nearby stood in the direct line of approach between the bank and the law office diagonally across the street. These were about to scuttle out of the way when Edge asked:

'Any of your regular deputies the liveryman, Sheriff?'

'What's that to you?' somebody growled aggressively, his voice pitched low like he needed to make the point but did not want to be identified.

Grimes answered Edge: 'Dave Doyle's a little old for that

24

kind of strenuous law work, mister.'

'Obliged if you'd have him take care of my horse? The roan gelding here at the rail. Feed, water and stabling is all. Pay Doyle when I know how many days I owe for.'

'Don't worry yourself about payin' for livery service, mister,' the lawman assured evenly. 'County'll take care of all your expenses while you're its guest.'

The group now split into two as Edge stepped off the sidewalk, started toward the law office. Behind him, perhaps the same man as before growled:

'And if the circuit judge sentences you to prison, or maybe to hang even, your horse and all you own'll be sold off to pay back the county!'

'You know somethin', John?' Harry Grimes said in a brittle tone as he moved up to be just a couple of paces behind Edge.

'I know lots, Harry.' There was a sudden note of unease in the voice now he had been named.

'If your brain was a quarter the size of your mouth, maybe once in awhile you'd say somethin' worth hearin'.' Then he evened out his tone to instruct: 'That's it, Edge. The jail is right over there across the street. Buildin' with the three barred windows. Keep doin' just like you're told and it could turn out you have a pleasant stay in our town.'

Edge made no reply, kept his lips compressed into a thin line as his slitted, glinting eyes scanned the length of Lark Street: paid closer attention to detail when he first rode along it. Not seeking a means of immediate escape, although if an opportunity occurred he might have taken it. Rather, he impressed on his mind a map of the small, neat town that might prove of use in the near future.

He saw another knot of curious people out near the western end of the street, one of them holding a saddled horse. Guessed this was where one of the men who held up the bank had been blasted out of his saddle and captured.

Once more he ignored the watching eyes, few of the local citizens making any attempt at surreptitiousness now, as they saw for certain—in their own minds—a man who had indeed turned out to be the bad lot he appeared when he first showed up in their quiet little town.

The law office was granite built like the bank but with three barred windows and a larger one fitted with frosted glass, and no sidewalk out front. As Edge drew near, the door beside the glazed window was jerked open and a fresh-faced youngster of sixteen or seventeen stepped on to the threshold. Although he toted a Winchester rifle, he looked nervous of Edge; tried to conceal this anxiety behind a sheepish smile he directed past the half-breed at Grimes.

'Figured you could use a little help with a guy mean-looking as this one, Sheriff. I hope you don't mind I got things ready here? So you can run him right on through into a cell I opened up. That okay?'

It was clear the sandy-haired, grey-eyed, gawky-framed youngster was prepared for either criticism or praise. And his smile faltered, then broadened into a grin when Grimes assured:

'You did fine, Nick. Appreciate it.'

They were all inside the law office by then. In a square, cramped room with a block of three cells off to the side, each partitioned from its neighbour by bars. Access to the cell doors was by means of a passageway between the rear stone wall of the building and the wall of bars.

Like the bank—and the exteriors of every building Edge recalled in any detail—the combined law office and jailhouse was clean, functional, almost spartan, but adequate for its purpose. It was much colder in there than over at the bank, the corner stove unlit.

'This way, mister,' Nick instructed, waved the Winchester then backed down the passage, gestured with the rifle again for Edge to enter the cell adjacent to the office. The door was ready open, the key in the lock. It had the usual basic facilities of a narrow cot with a thin mattress on top, a bucket beneath.

'You're still doing fine, kid,' Edge said as he stepped into the cell, turned and lowered himself gingerly on to the side of the cot. Was only now aware of the bruised knees he had suffered from the heavy fall behind the bank counter when the shooting started. He shared a cold-eyed gaze between both his captors as the kid banged the cell door closed, twisted the key in the lock, withdrew it. 'But either of you

26

aims a gun at me again, I'll kill you.'

'You're making me shake with fright, mister!' Nick countered sneeringly, exuding mounting confidence now the prisoner was safely locked in the cell.

'Another lesson in bein' a peace officer, Nick,' Grimes said earnestly as he holstered his revolver, went to a rifle rack with one empty slot where the kid had obviously gotten the Winchester.

'Yeah, Sheriff?'

Grimes instructed wearily: 'A man behind bars wants to shoot off his mouth, ain't no harm in that. Not much else he can do. There anythin' else you want, Edge? Apart from out of there?'

'For you to get a posse raised and get after those old-timers robbed the bank, Sheriff.'

The kid growled: 'If you're short of company, the guy Sam Parker winged'll be here soon as the doc has him patched up.'

'What I'm short of is a Colt revolver and a hundred and fifty bucks owed to somebody, kid,' Edge replied as he swung his legs up on the cot and lowered his back in the other direction. Then he tipped his hat forward over his face, blocked out of his eyes the failing light of the fall sun which angled in through the bars above his head.

Grimes sighed, muttered: 'Lesson number one hundred and a whole lot I guess, Nick. Never taunt a prisoner who comes quietly and behaves himself. It's liable to rile him and that's liable to backfire on you later.'

'Sure, Sheriff.'

'Edge?'

'Yeah?' he said through his hat.

'You say they're all old-timers? Like the one was shot ... He looks to be seventy if he's a day.'

'Didn't see the one called Duff,' the half-breed replied. 'The one that held the horses outside. But if any of the others were under seventy, won't be by many years, I'd guess.'

'Appreciate it,' Grimes said flatly, and Edge neither knew nor cared right then if the lawman gave credence to the implication he had never seen any of the bank robbers until today.

27

Then, as footfalls marked the lawman's progress toward the doorway while Edge remained blinded by the hat over his face, he said: 'You want fuller descriptions, Sheriff, talk with anyone was in the saloon the same time as the oldsters.'

There was an abruptness to the way Grimes halted. 'What's that about the saloon?'

'Five horses were hitched to the rail outside the Centennial when I rode into town. I don't guess a bunch of men fixing to rob the bank would've worn marks while they were drinking in the saloon next door.'

'Damn!' Grimes snapped. 'Nick, you're deputised!'

'Gee, thanks, Sheriff!' Huskily.

'See to it the other prisoner's locked up securely when he gets here! Watch the both of them and whatever they say or do, don't open the cell doors. Be back soon as I can with the rest of the gang.'

'Sure thing, Sheriff!' the kid blurted eagerly. 'Don't you worry none about me doing my duty.'

'Appreciate it,' Grimes said absently, stepped outside, closed the door behind him.

Edge closed his eyes under the hat, listened to the silence within the office for a few seconds. Then heard a drawer slide open, and Nick vent a grunting noise of pleasure. And the half-breed was intrigued enough to lift the brim of his Stetson, swivel his eyes to the limit of their sockets so he could peer out through the side wall of bars into the office area of the chill filled building.

The youngster was seated in the padded chair behind the desk which had just the Winchester on it, applying fascinated concentration to the simple task of pinning a deputy's badge to the left side of his jacket that was a mismatch for his pants: both items of clothing either grown out of or under-size reach-me-downs.

A moment later his attention was diverted by the sounds of horses on the street to the east, along with indistinct exchanges of talk. And he rose hurriedly, got halfway to the door and stopped with a low curse. Swung around, returned to retrieve the Winchester he had forgotten.

Edge let the hat drop back over his face as the kid cracked open the door: wide enough to watch the posse gallop away.

28

Some of the dust raised by the horse's pumping hooves drifted in on the cold evening air through the doorway and barred windows.

When the clatter of the hard-ridden horses had diminished into the distant west, riders and mounts doubtless lost in the billowing cloud of their own dust, Nick closed the door, crossed the office and dropped heavily—like he was disgruntled—into the chair behind the desk.

The town was very quiet after this, and inside the law office and jailhouse the stillness in the fading light of late afternoon was almost palpable. The air that infiltrated through the barred windows felt considerably colder than before in this near complete silence.

From under his hat, Edge said: 'I've heard most kids these days plan on being locomotive engineers when they're old enough.'

'What?' Nick sounded like he was startled out of a deep reverie. 'Oh, yeah, maybe a lot are like that. But not me, mister. It's plain I'm fixin' to be a peace officer, uh?'

'Right. I've seen you practising. It's a damn shame.'

'I guess a guy like you are has good reason not to like lawmen,' he sneered.

'It's not that, kid. Just if you had wanted to be an engineer you'd maybe have to start as a fireman? And you could practise by stoking some heat out of that cold stove in the corner.'

Nick snapped: 'I get cold enough, I'll do that thing, mister!'

'You're the boss.'

'Yeah, that's what I am! And you better remember it. That way, I reckon we'll get along just fine and dandy.'

Edge sighed, muttered: 'Be more warming to think of us getting along like a house on fire, kid.'

'Whatever.' He uttered a scornful grunt, then sneered: 'Oh, yeah, I get it! That was supposed to be some kinda lousy joke you just made, uh?'

Edge sighed again into the underside of his hat, thrust his hands deep into the pockets of the sheepskin coat, growled wryly: 'Right, kid. A joke. Just like your Pa and Ma once made.'

29

4

Nick got it wrong about the wounded member of the gang of old-timers providing company when he was patched up and locked in the jailhouse: the second prisoner was out cold when two men carried him into the building.

Before this Edge had not been tempted to drift into sleep while the small town went about its late afternoon and early evening business following the shock and excitement of the bank robbery. Even though the sounds of this end of the day activity were no more obtrusive than the occasional clop of slow-moving hooves, every now and then the creaking of a passing wagon, the far-off barking of a dog, the distant weary reprimanding shout of a harassed mother at a badly behaved child. Sometimes the dragging footfalls of Nick when he left the chair behind the desk, went to the door, opened it and peered out. Often accompanied his survey of the quiet street with a deep sigh of dissatisfaction, maybe boredom, that revealed he regretted his eagerly given promise to remain on guard.

Once or twice when this happened, Edge almost growled a demand the door be closed, to block off the draught of chill air. Too, the aroma of woodsmoke, later mixed with cooking fragrances, that added the ache of hunger to the discomfort of being cold. But he held back from voicing the complaint: reasoned the kid, being the churlish kind, was likely to keep the door open longer just to spite the prisoner.

It never did remain open for much more than a minute or so: until he saw something to concern him as a deputy. And Edge wriggled up into a seated attitude, leaned his back against the wall at the head of the cot, started to roll a cigarette when the kid called:

'Evening to you, Doc Salmon! Mr Doyle! Sheriff's

deputised me and I'm to see both prisoners stay safe and sound here.'

Two sets of footfalls drew close to the open doorway.

'Well, this one will no' cause you any trouble for some time to come, laddie,' one of the men responded in a broad Scottish accent. He sounded a little breathless.

The kid turned from the door, excited to be occupied with active law business again. Hurried to the desk, jerked open a drawer, scooped out a key and entered the passageway to unlock the door of the cell next to the one in which he only now realised Edge was no longer sprawled out on the cot, face beneath his hat, apparently asleep.

'One of your partners in crime's being brought in,' he blurted.

Edge struck a match on the wall behind him, lit the fresh-rolled cigarette, said on a stream of exhaled smoke: 'Didn't the sheriff get to the lesson about a man being innocent until proved guilty under US law, kid?'

Nick scowled, had no time to rasp a response before the town doctor and liveryman entered. The city-suited Scotsman was gripping the shoulders and the leather-aproned Doyle held the ankles of the limply curved prisoner. One of the men smelled of antiseptic, another of horses, and somebody of cheap whiskey. From the way he breathed and snored in a stupor rather than a natural sleep, the whiskey smell came off the prisoner. It was not an agreeable combination of smells, and Edge worked at creating a dense cloud of aromatic tobacco smoke that went some way to masking it.

After the two men had carried their burden into the cell, set the unconscious man down on the cot with a clumsy kind of gentleness, Nick asked anxiously:

'He gonna be okay, Doc?'

The tic in the left cheek of the unconscious man named him as the elderly bank robber called Pete. In his present condition there were no spasms in his left side: but perhaps this was because of the constriction of the dressing that bulked out his clothing in this area.

'At present the man is dead drunk on the bottle and a half

31

of whiskey I was required to pour into him so that I could extract the bullet from his side,' Salmon answered. 'This will no doubt keep him anaesthetised for some little time to come.'

The doctor was fifty or so, short and slightly built, with a neat grey moustache and short cut black hair.

'Damn sorry waste of good liquor to my mind,' said the sixty plus Doyle, heavily built, spade bearded and dull eyed. Addressing the opinion to Edge: who said, 'You take good care of my horse before you go get your share of anaesthetic, feller.'

Doyle seemed not to hear, his mind maybe still totally occupied with resentful thoughts concerned with the wasted whiskey.

Salmon eyed his surroundings bleakly: including the other three men and the youngster who featured in them. Then demanded with a grimace: 'Are there no blankets for the cell beds, young Cornwall?'

The kid said hurriedly, defensively: 'The sheriff didn't say nothing about that, Doc. Just told me to see the prisoners were kept safe and sound until he got back with the rest of the bank robbers.'

'Well, they need blankets this time of the year, laddie. And get a fire lit in that stove. It's positively freezing in this place.'

The youngster allowed sullenly: 'If you say so, Doc.'

'I do say so, laddie! I have ensured the man who was in my care does not die from the gunshot wound he received. I can assure you the tales that alcohol warms the blood are total fallacy. So unless you get some warmth in here, he could freeze to death and my labours will have been in vain. I do not like to work toward such an end.'

He let his small, bright eyes rest on Edge for a moment, asked: 'Are you all right?'

'I've been in worse jailhouses, Doc,' the half-breed told him. 'And if the kid heats it up like you tell him, it could go down as one of my best.' He looked at Doyle who had moved toward the doorway, reminded the liveryman: 'About my horse, feller?'

The man responded with a non-commital grunt as he

32

stepped out of the building. Salmon started to follow, then paused to assure:

'You've no worry on that score. David Doyle attends to horses better than most people treat other people.' He looked sharply at the youngster who was moving away from the cells, going toward the desk, said sternly: 'Get that stove lit, laddie. And I will see to it blankets are supplied by the hotel. If there is any change for the worse in the patient's condition, let me know at once.'

'I sure will do... that, you know-it-all old sonofabitch!'

Nick Cornwall, who bore no family resemblance in face or build to the big woman who almost caused panic at the bank in the wake of the robbery, altered what he intended to say—and the tone of the voice in which he said it—after the doctor had hurried out of the law office, banged the door behind him.

Edge growled: 'That's fine, kid. Being polite to people who aren't other lawmen isn't on the list of rules for lawmen.'

Nick again dropped heavily into the chair behind the desk. Slammed the rifle down on the empty desk top. Stared into a middle distance with a soured expression that conveyed he didn't like what he saw there. But he did not entirely withdraw into the private world of dissatisfaction. After perhaps ten seconds he surfaced from it, complained:

'I want to hear any damn thing from you, mister, I'll tell you! Okay?'

It was hard not to give in to an impulse to snarl an angry response: for a full grown man considerably more than twice the age of the kid to react with puerile resentment to what was said by Cornwall. But it would have served little purpose, except as a temporary easy outlet for the build-up of latent anger Edge had suppressed ever since he turned and saw Donna Terry aiming the old Colt revolver at him: realised at that instant exactly how it had to look to her.

Which was exactly how she had started to tell it to the impatient local sheriff.

Not for the first time in his life he had ridden into the wrong town at the wrong time, and now he was tightly enmeshed in a trap of circumstantial evidence which implicated him in the

33

bank robbery pulled off by the bunch of old men highly skilled at what they were doing. Had fallen foul of the law in a way the people of Munro could only take his stranger's word he was an innocent victim of circumstances, or go along with everything else that pointed directly to his guilt.

He glanced through the bars at the frail-looking old man sprawled on the cot in the next cell. Knew from the way he breathed so deeply and regularly, Pete would certainly recover from the gunshot wound. But the old-timer was not going to surface from the drunkard's sleep for awhile yet. Even when he did, though, proclaimed he had no knowledge of Edge until today, was it likely he would be believed? Get Edge turned loose? Fat chance!

Too, the half-breed reasoned as he absently switched his incurious gaze to the youthful deputy who fed kindling and cordwood into the stove, then started a fire in the grate, even if the other four members of the gang were rounded up, their joint assertions he was not one of their number might not be believed. At least until a trial, which was some way off.

After he was through smoking the cigarette, he crushed out the butt, resumed his relaxed attitude on the cot. With his hat over his face, now relished the first warmth from the stove. Soon found the regular breathing of the man in the neighbouring cell soporific, was on the verge of sleep when the law office door opened suddenly.

He looked out from under his hat in time to see Nick Cornwall half rise, snatch up the Winchester from the desk, aim it at the doorway, too scared to vent a sound through the wide gape of his mouth.

Edge smelled chilli and shifted his gaze toward the doorway as the squeaky-voiced man named Vaughan blurted anxiously:

'My goodness, Nicky! You almost made me drop the food. Pointin' the rifle at me that way.'

The kid gulped, countered grimly: 'Damnit, you oughta have knocked, called out who it was, Mr Jameson!' His tone became a whine when he added: 'And don't call me Nicky no more! I'm past the age for that kinda stupid kid's name!'

'Now you're old enough to cuss in front of an innocent

34

young child?' Vaughan Jameson accused as he approached the desk, set down a tray covered with a cloth from beneath which steam, appetisingly laced with the aroma of chilli, escaped.

He was closely followed by a slightly built, dark haired and dark eyed, solemn faced girl of eight or nine. She carried a pile of folded blankets which Jameson turned and took from her.

'He . . . well,' Cornwall started to curse, managed to correct himself with a shake of his head. 'Sheriff's left me in charge to guard these prisoners. It stands to reason I'm going to get a little hot and bothered, people just come barging in here without announcing who they are. You could've been any——'

'All right, all right,' Jameson cut in, put the blankets down on the desk beside the tray. Then draped an arm around the narrow shoulders of the small girl who leaned in close to him. 'Doc Salmon called at the hotel, asked Mrs Wilde to cook hot food, provide some blankets for the prisoners. Here it all is. Leave you to do your duty of carin' for the prisoners, Nicky—sorry, Nick. Force of habit.'

As he turned with his arm still draped around the small girl to steer her toward the open doorway, he found his suddenly nervous eyes trapped by the steady gaze of Edge. And he sounded as rattled as he looked when he almost stuttered: 'Goodnight to you, stranger.'

Edge nodded, acknowledged: 'That food tastes as good as it smells, it's sure going to improve the night for me, feller.'

Jameson nodded vigorously. 'Enjoy. Come along, Ellen, let's go.'

The little girl walked somewhat reluctantly beside him, then summoned up the nerve to say reproachfully to the half-breed: 'I had two dollars and thirty seven cents saved up in Aunt Donna's bank, sir.'

Edge felt uncomfortably lost for words for a stretched second as he watched the man and child near the doorway. Then he nodded, told her: 'I figure that's just what it's worth to me for you to bring me the blankets on such a cold night, little lady.'

He rolled on to one side, pulled up the other side of the sheepskin coat, delved into a pants pocket for some coins.

The solemn eyes of the girl suddenly lit with an eager smile, until Vaughan Jameson hurried her ahead of him out of the law office, held back for a moment to tell Edge:

'No offence intended, mister. But Ellen doesn't do chores for anythin' more than the ten cents I already paid her. If her money isn't gotten back from them who stole it, then she'll have to take the loss the same way as the rest of us who had savin's in the bank. Night to you again.'

As soon as the door closed behind the earnest faced, squeaky voiced man, Cornwall lifted the cloth off the tray, and softly vented a more obscene curse than he spoke in the hearing of the small girl.

Edge said: 'Nothing smells so good as that can be that bad, kid.'

Cornwall shook his head, complained: 'Only thing wrong with it, there's just the two bowls of grub, mister. Mary Wilde forgot I have to eat, too.'

Edge swung his feet to the floor, jerked a thumb over his shoulder toward the sleeping man in the next cell. 'Be a time before he's ready for food, kid.'

'Hey, that's right, damnit!' He grinned and rose from the desk, brought a bowl of chilli with a spoon in it, set it on the floor and leaned back from the door to slide it into Edge's cell with the toe of his boot.

Edge had picked up the bowl, started to discover just how good was the food before Cornwall got back to the desk.

For a few minutes the law office was noisy with the sounds of the two of them eating and the breathing of the sleeping Pete.

Soon after the food was eaten a clock some way down the street chimed six and Cornwall took this as a signal to bring the blankets to the cells, pushed two under each door. Now his belly was full and he had recovered from the fleeting moments of resentment when he thought he would have to go hungry, he worked at being tough again. Toted the Winchester with him and did not lean back so far when he pushed the bedding into Edge's cell with a foot.

Edge would have had to lunge the full width of the cell to reach the youngster. Instead he remained seated on the cot with his back to the front wall of the building again as he rolled a cigarette. Idly watched the kid push the other blankets into the next cell, then return to the desk, set the rifle down on its top.

Cornwall leaned far enough back in the chair so he could rest his feet on the desk top. And interlocked the fingers of his hands behind his neck. Now looked totally in command of the situation, fully satisfied with his lot.

Edge sat and smoked, impassive behind the thin lipped, narrow eyed mask of his face, his mind involuntarily filled with memories from the recent past, thoughts of the future beyond the time when he was out of this cell, clear of Munro, free of the trouble that had trapped him here.

Memories of Nancy Raven, the whore who impulsively loaned him the money for a trip to the Providence River Valley in California. Where, rumour had it, Adam Steele had set himself up as a horse rancher, was doing fine at it.

Just as impulsively, Edge had changed direction. Headed south instead of west. Ridden down into the native land of his long dead father: with not such a clear cut aim as he had in his mind when he told Nancy Raven why he wanted to go see the Virginian's horse ranch.

In his lifetime he had come across a score—hell, maybe even as many as a hundred—men like Adam Steele. Like himself, damnit! Drifting saddletramps who lived from one day to the next without making plans: existed on their wits and survived by their skills with the gun.

The kind of hardbitten free spirits who, he had always thought, were inevitably destined to die young in one final eruption of violence. When a faster man with a gun or an accident of unkind fate meant they went down on some strange piece of dirt where they were as likely to be left as buzzard meat as to be buried in an unmarked grave.

Or, just maybe, they had the luck—good or bad?—to live to a ripe old age. Die in a strange bed under a roof not their own. Or in a bedroll under the stars. Unmourned: their end maybe even welcomed by strangers who considered the lives they had led a useless waste.

But, rumour had it, Adam Steele had been able to change the course of his life. So was unique as far as Edge knew, in how he had reached the compromise of a piece of land, a long way from his native Virginia, where he could put down roots. Build the kind of business he desired. Live in a community where every eye did not nervously follow his progress along the street, expecting trouble to explode around him.

Rumours were all Edge had heard. But he found these naggingly intriguing. And wondered often in the middle of some long, dark night in a strange town or in a camp beside some stretch of lonesome trail, if such a life were right for him.

Nothing so grandiose as a horse ranch.

A little farmstead: like the one he had been raised on in Iowa, or the place he had shared for such a tragically short time with Beth in the Dakotas.

But where now? In his father's adopted country of the United States? Or down across the border in Mexico?

He had spent a lot of years riding the trails of the country of his birth. Had not often responded to the insistent tug on that half of his bloodline that stretched into Mexico. So it had seemed like a good idea when he rode out of Cheyenne with the whore's money in his pocket to take another look across the border.

A drifter who felt the need to call a halt had to be sure he picked the right spot.

Or had the long detour into Mexico simply been an excuse not to go to California when he at last had the money to finance the trip? Because, deep down inside he was afraid of what he might find at the Trail's End spread in the Providence River Valley? Where Adam Steele had located his piece of paradise on earth. Been long enough there to establish something good: something it was too late for Edge to try to emulate.

Just how would he feel toward Steele who had broken the basic rule of life he had always lived by—Edge still did—that a man with nothing had nothing to lose.

Was he afraid of what he would feel? Envy, jealousy, frustration, resentment, anger? Or some kind of jaundiced sense of superiority toward a one-time hard man gone soft now there were no longer potential dangers lurking in every street doorway, behind every outcrop of rock along the open trail?

He wouldn't feel anything good, he was certain in his own mind of that: but he had to go take a look.

Maybe he'd find out the rumours were untrue: or the sweet-sounding set-up had turned sour on Steele since Edge first heard tell of the Virginian's success in the Providence River Valley.

But if life was still good for Steele, and Edge felt moved to attempt something similar, at least now he had the wherewithal to get started. Which was not the case when he switched directions out of Cheyenne with just travelling money borrowed from the whore in his pants pocket. Now he had the bounty on the Railton brothers, unwittingly earned out of the trouble that started in San Cristobel after the Mexican trip. Which was enough to pay the debt due Nancy Raven, finance a trip to California, leave a balance of several hundred dollars toward starting up in business.

If that was what he wanted.

North or south of the border?

That didn't matter right then: because he didn't know what the hell he wanted, damnit!

'What's that you say, mister?'

A ceiling-hung kerosene lamp had been lit while Edge allowed his mind the freedom to wander along a line of thought that had evidently caused him to utter an involuntary exclamation. In its light he looked sharply across at the kid, saw surprise on the youthful face.

'Shit, why're you looking at me like that?' Cornwall asked tautly, shock suddenly etched deeply into his immature features.

The half-breed now became aware of the rigidity of his own face. Knew from past experience, as he recognised the significance of his surroundings and circumstances, his features had formed into the scowl that always spread across them when he had reason to hate whoever or whatever he looked at.

This time it was different: his own feelings were what he

despised so vehemently. And eventually he said wearily: 'No sweat, kid. It wasn't you I was looking at.'

He rasped a hand over a day-long growth of bristles, touched the scabbed scar of the scratch Donna Terry opened on his cheek. Wondered briefly if the dark line of congealed blood gave his scowling face an even more frightening aspect in the lamp's fringe glow that reached into the cell.

'Mister, I . . .' Cornwall started to rasp. Shook his head and worked some saliva into his throat which was dried by fear. Managed to complete in a rush: 'I sure am glad about that!'

Edge expressed a glinting-eyed grin as he wriggled up into a sitting position with his back against the wall. Said evenly: 'The spot I'm in right now, kid, I'll go along with you either way.'

Nick Cornwall blinked and shook his head in perplexity, grunted: 'Uh?'

Edge drawled: 'The sentence. Not finished or over real fast.'

5

Nick Cornwall expressed the kind of weak smile that Edge figured was better than the poor joke was worth. And, the half-breed thought, the expression had more to do with a sense of relief than anything else.

But then the kid switched his gaze from the cell to the door of the law office as it opened: and the look of relief was abruptly displaced by greater shock than before as he groaned: 'Oh, no!'

The croaking-voiced bank robber named Gene countered grimly: 'Don't tell me no, kid! And don't move even your eyes toward that there rifle on the desk. Else you'll reach the Promised Land way ahead of your time, son.'

The lenses of his wire-framed spectacles glinted in the lamplight as he stepped over the threshold, Colt thrust forward from his hip. Like at the bank, a kerchief mask hid his lower face.

Cornwall made a low, inarticulate sound that just managed to squeeze out from his fear constricted throat.

'That kinda sounded like another no to me, kid,' Gene warned as he closed the door behind him. He glanced toward the cells, did a double-take at Edge seated nonchalantly on the cot in the nearest one.

Pete remained deeply asleep in the neighbouring cell.

A more experienced deputy might have used the stretched seconds of Gene's careless surprise to snatch up the Winchester, blast a shot at the old-timer. Taken a chance on the other old men not being close enough to retaliate. But Nick Cornwall remained paralysed with terror by what was happening.

'What the hell d'you do wrong, mister?' Gene croaked. Now remembered to check on the kid before he advanced on the desk, dragged the Winchester off it by the muzzle end, dropped it noisily on the floor.

Edge replied: 'Obliged if you'd tell the kid here—and anyone else you happen to run into—I didn't do anything wrong: far as you and your partners know.'

'What?' He shook his head, scowled. 'What the hell? I don't have the time for riddles.' Now he waved the gun at Cornwall, commanded: 'Get a key and let Pete Race outta his cell, kid.'

The youngster vented another inarticulate sound. His Adam's apple was the only part of him that moved. Until the old-timer leaned over the desk, would have pushed the muzzle of the Colt into the centre of Cornwall's forehead had not the youngster vented a low squeal, leaned away from the revolver.

'That's the way,' Gene rasped, his eyes behind the lenses glinting with sardonic humour. 'Best you bend over backwards to help me, kid. Because if I have to do things myself, it'll likely be over your dead body.'

The youngster swallowed hard again, nodded vigorously. Was now able to haul himself to his feet and start toward the space between the line of cells and the rear wall of the building.

Edge reminded him: 'You forgot the key.'

Cornwall looked sick to his stomach, glanced at Gene like he feared the oversight would count fatally against him. Then he turned, jerked open a drawer of the desk. Gasped as the muzzle of the revolver pressed hard into his temple. A muffled sound, then a rancid stench manifested just how frightened he was.

Gene pulled a face, leaned forward to peer into the drawer, said: 'Sorry to scare you shitless that way, son. But maybe that guy was steerin' you to a gun.' He hardened his tone to snap: 'Okay, go unlock Pete Race's cell!'

Gene went on ahead, backed into the passageway, so he was close to where his partner slept, could attempt to wake Race without the need to shout too loud.

'Hey, you lazy bastard, Pete! Wake up, old buddy! You're gettin' outta here!'

Cornwall fumbled with the key, finally got it inserted in the lock. Turned it as Gene peered long and hard at the sleeping form in the dark cell beyond the reach of the light from the kerosene lamp.

'What's wrong with Pete?' he demanded. Swung his gaze from Cornwall to Edge and back at Race. 'He's hurt so bad, he didn't oughta be locked in a friggin' jail!'

'The Doc had to——' Cornwall started to reply, until his throat dried up on him again when Gene shouldered him clear of the doorway, lunged into the cell, crouched beside the cot.

Edge snarled: 'Don't be crazy, kid. He's got a gun!'

Cornwall had made to reach for the cell door, slam it closed. Maybe would have gotten the key turned in the lock before Gene whirled and fired.

Gene did spin around as he straightened up, swung the gun and came within the shortest part of a second of squeezing the trigger before he was able to freeze his forefinger. His mind worked as fast as his physical responses, for he said without need of an instant's pause for thought:

'Open the other guy's cage, kid.'

He stepped out of the cell as the malodorous youngster now moved almost as quickly to obey the command as Gene had been to issue it. Used the same key which fitted both locks.

Then Edge remained seated with his back to the front wall of the jailhouse, watched through slitted eyes under hooded lids as Gene shepherded Cornwall into the law office section of the building again. Held the revolver muzzle hard against the nape of the youngster's neck.

The two halted alongside the desk and the Colt continued to be held against bristled flesh as Gene turned to peer at Edge, asked:

'No matter why a man's locked up in jail, he always wants out, I figure?'

Edge replied: 'Especially so when he's not guilty of the crime they locked him up for, feller.'

Gene sighed. 'I guess you don't give much of a damn about the life of this boy?'

'We haven't exactly been getting on like a house on fire.'

Nick Cornwall gulped, groaned, trembled.

Gene nodded, but left the gun muzzle where it was. 'I didn't plan on Pete Race bein' out for the count the way he is.'

'It's mostly the liquor they poured down his throat to kill the pain so the local doctor could dig the bullet out of his side, feller,' Edge supplied.

'Obliged for the information, mister.' He sounded genuinely grateful, then anxious when he went on: 'Be obliged again if you'll lend me the hand I need gettin' him outta here?' Suddenly thought to add: 'Recall how you feel about havin' guns aimed at you, and I ain't doin' it, am I? Aimin' this here gun at you?'

Edge placed his feet on the floor but remained seated on the cot as he answered: 'If your end includes giving me back my gun and the hundred and fifty bucks I'd deposited in the bank just before you and your partners robbed it, we got a deal.'

Gene scowled, countered sullenly: 'I ain't got your gun nor any money with me right now, frig it!'

'Later'll be fine. But the sooner the better.'

'Then we got us a deal, mister.' His tone had lightened and his eyes sparkled with relief behind the spectacle lenses.

'Much obliged,' Edge responded as he rose to his feet, moved out of his cell and into the one next door.

For the first time since Nick Cornwall had been so badly frightened, he smelled the stale whiskey on the breath of Pete Race. This as he stooped over the cot, lifted the slightly built old-timer, draped him face down over a shoulder. Took care not to bang the man's unfeeling head against the bars as he crossed the threshold of the cell.

'That's fine,' Gene said, now withdrew the gun muzzle from the neck of the terrified youngster. 'Best I show myself at the doorway first. On account of Ruben and Rich see you totin' Pete like he's a side of beef, they could maybe get the wrong idea?'

'You're the boss, feller,' Edge muttered.

As Gene moved toward the door, the half-breed looked pointedly at Cornwall, sagged against the front of the desk. But the eyes of the bad smelling youngster were squeezed tightly closed as he struggled to retain a fragile grip on himself: fought off being sick to his stomach, maybe even passing out. So he was in no frame of mind to see, let alone understand the tacit signal from Edge that he should try to reclaim the Winchester that lay on the floor nearby.

For a reckless moment, Edge considered launching the lightweight Race at the man near the door. Then lunging to scoop up the Winchester. Knew he would need to pump the action of the repeater to be sure there was a bullet in the breech before he squeezed the trigger.

But the next instant he rejected the notion. The risk was not worth taking right there and then, when he was getting out of the Munro jailhouse without need to put his life on the line anyway.

So he started to move slowly after Gene, still primed to recognise an opportunity to escape in a situation when a calculated chance was worth taking.

The bespectacled old-timer started to open the door when Edge had closed to within a few feet of him. And at that precise moment there came a sharp sound from behind them. Over near the desk.

Both of them whirled. Saw Nick Cornwall down on his knees, torso canted forward as his hands swung toward the Winchester on the floor in front of him.

'Damn fool, kid!' Gene rasped thickly, squeezed the trigger of the Colt.

The bullet tunnelled into the side of Cornwall's head in front of the right ear. Hit him over a short range with a force of impact that twisted his body, slammed it hard against the front of the desk. A moment later the kid with the lawman's badge pinned to his too-tight suit jacket was sprawled out on his side, his inert form covering the stock of the rifle.

Edge knew the instant he heard the shot that the Winchester was not the reason Nick Cornwall was down on his knees. For the half-breed clearly saw what the near-sighted eyes of the panicked Gene failed to recognise.

The youngster's face was chalk white and his eyes started to roll up in their sockets, glazed over, as the lids closed, the mouth fell slackly open. Shame, terror, humiliation and whatever other dark emotions had affected the kid in the tense period since Gene entered the law office had combined to plunge him toward the unconsciousness of a faint.

'I friggin' warned him!' Gene complained grimly, wrenched the door open wide. 'He should've believed me, dammit!'

Edge swept his impassive gaze from the dead youngster to Gene. Then beyond the threshold to the area of street out front of the law office. Where Ruben leaned on his polished black cane and Rich stood awkwardly on his stiff leg: each of the old-timers in process of hurriedly jerking up a kerchief to cover his lower face.

'He couldn't do that, seems to me,' the half-breed muttered sardonically through pursed lips. 'This whole bunch of desperadoes is just unbelievable.'

6

A wagon started to hurtle along the street from the west, the sounds of its frenetic progress shattering the tense silence of the night that followed the gunshot. Then a crackle of gunfire exploded out of the same direction, counterpointing the thudding of galloping hooves and clatter of fast-spinning wheels.

Ruben started to ask a question as both he and Rich let go of their kerchiefs which slid off their chins as they reached to draw their handguns, swung them toward Edge.

'He's with us!' Gene snarled, side-stepped to place his skinny frame in front of the half-breed, partially shielding him from the levelled revolvers. 'Let's get the frig outta here!'

'That's just what we're gonna do, good buddy!' Ruben yelled, thrust his stick high in the air, whirled toward the approaching wagon. Began to roar for the driver to speed up, his bellowing voice surely lost to the man with the reins against the barrage of gunfire that spat muzzle flashes and spurts of smoke from out of the dust cloud raised by the racing rig.

Then Ruben and Rich used their Colts, directed a fusillade of shots along the eastern stretch of Lark Street.

There were long moments, while raucous noise filled the night and attention was concentrated elsewhere, when Edge had the chance to alter the course of action he chose to follow after Nick Cornwall went down, spilling his life blood.

The Winchester was still on the floor, half under the kid's corpse, and once more there was opportunity to dump Pete Race, get a hand on the rifle. But he instinctively knew the time was still not right.

Then the wagon made a spectacular halt out front of the law office. After the driver held the team at a flat out gallop until the last moment, then hauled on the reins, wrenched on the brakes. The locked wheels and slithering hooves raised a thicker and higher cloud of billowing dust, impenetrable to the shaft of lamplight that angled from the law office doorway.

Edge stepped out of the building as the protesting snorts of the abused team animals added to the cacophony of discordant sounds: three of the old-timers yelling incoherently while they continued to loose off shots along the street. Aimed at nothing palpable: the purpose of the gunfire to persuade the citizens of Munro it was wise to stay inside, keep their heads down while the jailbreak was accomplished.

Gene did not fire his Colt. But he kept it drawn as he yelled at Edge: 'On the back with him, mister!'

He turned to help with hefting the unfeeling form of the drunkenly torpid Race on to the rear of the flatbed wagon.

The revolvers of Ruben and Rich rattled empty and they thrust them into their holsters, clambered clumsily aboard the wagon. There snatched up rifles, repeaters like the one Duff was firing from up on the driver's seat. And immediately a louder, more rapid fire barrage was laid down: the racket sounding almost like that from a Gatling gun.

Gene hauled himself on to the flatbed, was now as disinterested in Edge as the other members of the gang. And the half-breed, brightly illuminated in the light from the open door of the law office now the dust had settled, again thought fleetingly about turning and ducking into the relative safety of the building.

But his mind suddenly filled with a vivid image of the kid's body lying there: the only witness to what had happened during the jail break. Knew he was no better off than before: worse, since there had been a killing.

Some of the townspeople were starting to respond to the barrage of gunfire with sporadic shots of their own. A bullet cracked close enough to Edge for him to feel the draught of its slipstream across a cheek before he heard the thud as it was buried in the timber of the doorframe behind him.

Ruben roared in high excitement: 'Let's go, Duff!'

'Get aboard, stranger!' Gene yelled and his tone made it

more a command than an urgent plea.

'Goddamnit, move her on outta here!' Rich snarled. He was plainly scared.

The wagon jolted forward and Edge hurled himself toward its moving rear. Would maybe not have made it had not clawed hands reached out to grasp the scruff of the neck of his sheepskin coat, then hooked an armpit, next clutched the leg he swung up.

Thus was he dragged painfully on to the juddering bed of the wagon as Duff steered it into an abrupt tight turn. Started to race the rig back the way it had come as a hail of bullets was blasted after it: thudded into the timbers and richocheted off its metal parts. Fired by people who mostly stayed in moon-shadowed cover, shooting blind at the moving billow of dust again raised by the racing rig.

Duff now concentrated entirely on driving the wagon, keeping it on a straight, high-speed course along the centre of Lark Street into the moon bright night.

But the rifle he had discarded was either on or under the seat: anyway was beyond the reach of Edge. As the other three old-timers sprawled across the rear of the bed of the wagon made violent use of their repeaters, exploded a constant barrage of shots back through the blinding curtain of trailing dust.

So there was nothing for Edge to do but protect himself as best he could while the battle raged around him: and he pressed his body as flat to the shuddering boards as possible. Face down, lengthwise, to narrow the target for wildly fired bullets cracking toward the wagon; head forward, feet to the rear.

Told himself a rifle, or any other kind of gun, would have been of little use to him then, anyway. Unless to fire high and wide into the night: to make it appear he was fully on the side of the old-timers. On the other hand, if he was suddenly seen to have acquired a weapon, it could have the opposite effect.

The high tension of the fear of sudden death amid the chaos of sound acted to stretch time, but Edge had plenty of experience of similar situations. He knew how real time could be warped by such circumstances, figured little more than a minute at the most had elapsed when the wagon raced clear of effective gunshot range. Thundered off the end of the town street and out on to open trail.

The people of Munro and the men aboard the rig quickly realised this. The shooting from the wagon faltered and ended first. And soon just pumping hooves and rattling wheels filled the night as the townspeople put up their guns, surely now converged cautiously on the law office, dreading what they would find there.

The four alert men on the rear of the cramped wagon raised their heads, looked around at each other and the unconscious Race, to see whether anyone had been hit by a stray bullet. Then anxious questions were shouted, relieved answers yelled against the clattering sounds of the fast-moving wagon.

It was Gene who crouched at the side of Race, reported the injured man seemed no worse than when he was loaded aboard.

Then Ruben pulled up a pants leg and vented a gust of laughter Gene and Rich found infectious.

This soon cackled loud enough to reach the ears of Duff, who shot a puzzled look down over his shoulder: only then realised he alone was still masked. He jerked the kerchief down over his chin, faced front again and hauled on the reins to slow the sweat-lathered team from the headlong pace. Then he peered back again, checked the trail through the thinning veil of dust behind the wagon. He failed to see any sign of pursuit and then surveyed the men on the wagon bed, paid particularly close attention to Edge: seeing him for the first time.

The half-breed had risen into a half sitting attitude, most of his weight on one folded leg while he braced himself with a hand and the other leg. Gained his first impression of the driver, then briefly studied the unmasked faces of the other old-timers who, with the exception of Race, adopted attitudes similar to his own.

Duff was seventy, give or take a year. Shorter and more heavily built than the others, which did not make him fat. He had the grey stubble of an embryo beard, or maybe he was unable or had been disinclined to shave for several days. His small eyes were deep set, seemed placed too close together. A prominent, crooked nose looked liked it had been broken more than once.

The stiff-legged Rich appeared maybe ten years younger than all his partners, but this impression could simply have been created by his full head of hair that had not greyed at all in later life. A bushy moustache that drooped unevenly to either side of a full-lipped mouth was also solid coloured in the glittering light of the half moon. His eyes, their colour indeterminate right then, reminded Edge of his own: slitted, cold looking under hooded lids. He was an inch under six feet tall, with a slender build.

The seventy or so, bespectacled Gene matched this height, but his frame suggested a greater sinewy strength. The line of his mouth, along with the glint of light on his glasses, gave his face a harder, meaner look than the rest: even the narrow-eyed Rich.

Ruben, also as near to seventy as made little difference, had a round, fleshy-faced head on an almost emaciated body: like he had endured a disease that wasted his torso and limbs, failed to affect the face under a head that was bald except for a horseshoe of curly grey hair around the back and sides of his domed skull. In his present good-humoured mood he looked avuncular as he raised the pants leg, displayed the way a bullet had gouged a large splinter out of the wooden limb.

The suddenly less evenly breathing Pete Race, who Edge now studied closely for the first time, was the ugliest of the bunch, with sharp, rodent-like features that included prominent top teeth. A livid scar from an old knife wound was inscribed from the centre of his right cheek to the point of his jaw. It seemed like his left cheek twitched more often as his condition worsened: if his irregular breathing was an indication of lessening strength.

All the men wore western style clothing, dark hued and long past its prime.

After Duff was through eyeing him mistrustfully at the start of the relative calm in the wake of the frenetic jailbreak, all the men ignored the presence of the half-breed among

51

them while they savoured the success of their second assault on the town of Munro.

Edge continued to survey them and thought their laughter was nearing the point of frenzied hysteria as they over-reacted to the harmless bullet hole in Ruben's wooden leg. And he decided this was a pointer to the degree of strain they were under during the jailbreak: made more intense by determination to conceal their feelings from each other.

Then Ruben suddenly ended his laughter, let the pants leg drop into place, peered levelly at Edge. This as the wagon rounded a curve, started on a downslope that carried it out of sight of Munro. He asked flatly:

'So, what's with this guy, Gene?'

'We made a deal, Rube.'

'You said.'

Rich moved between Edge and Race, interrupted anxious-ly: 'Hey, Pete sounds like he's in a bad way. And he sure looks it, too.'

'Be because of how he was tossed around, feller,' Edge said. 'Leaking blood again, could be.'

'Yeah,' Gene hurried to agree. 'Pete was sleepin' deep and easy in the jailhouse. Local doctor had to put him under with a couple of pints of hard liquor so he could get to work and dig the bullet outta him.'

'I can smell the rye on his breath!' Rich growled, sounded to Edge much like Dave Doyle, the Munro liveryman, a few hours ago—as if he deeply resented not having a share in the free whiskey. Then he pulled a face, held up a hand which in the moonlight was seen to be stained with the dark sheen of fresh blood. 'You guys sure did open up the bullet hole when you was bein' so——'

Gene cut in defensively: 'We had to get Pete outta there fast, Shelby! And, anyway, I reckon he'd rather have a little pain and be outta jail instead of restin' easy behind bars!'

'Damn right!' Duff agreed from up on the driver's seat. 'Rube, you want me to take it easy so the joltin' don't make things worse for Pete?'

'Hell, no!' the leader of the group countered. 'When the goin's right for the team, make time, good buddy. Better Pete

52

be in a whole lot of pain than the whole bunch of us get caught. What kinda deal was that, Gene?'

The bespectacled man had to pause for thought: recall what he said awhile go to invite the delayed query. Then he nodded, answered: 'Seems this guy put a hundred and fifty bucks in the bank just before we showed up and hit it, Rube. He wants his money back. And the gun you took off him at the bank.'

'For what?' the man with the fleshy face atop the emaciated body asked. 'In return, I mean?'

'You seen the shape Pete's in. And there was a kid lawman on guard in the jailhouse. I couldn't have kept the boy from stoppin' me while I hauled Pete outta there on my own. Needed a hand, and he lent it on them terms about the gun and the money.'

Ruben countered evenly: 'Seem to recall noticin' it wasn't just a signal shot you let off to bring the wagon down the street, Gene? Thought I saw someone—that kid lawman, I guess—with blood oozin' outta a hole in his head back there in the jailhouse?'

Gene's voice got a little shrill with temper when he argued: 'Hell, that was after, Rube! Damn fool kid tried to be a hero and I had to blast him. This guy was already helpin' me with Pete by then.'

'For his sixshooter and a hundred and fifty bucks?' Ruben said evenly, eyeing Edge quizzically, inviting him to contribute to the exchange.

'For my gun and *my* hundred and fifty bucks,' Edge amended with heavy stress the second time he used the pronoun.

'Hold on tight, you guys!' Duff warned, yelled at the team, then cracked the reins above their backs to demand another spurt of speed on a long straightway down a gentle incline toward an extensive stand of timber about a half mile distant.

Everyone heeded his advice to brace themselves. Shelby took it upon himself to steady the unconscious Race as the rig once more bucked and pitched and rolled at high speed on the rutted and pot-holed trail.

Edge sensed that everyone except the strenuously occupied

driver spared some degree of attention to watch him. Did not trust him to remain so seemingly quietly co-operative after doubt had been raised about the wisdom of Gene in allowing the stranger along.

Close to the expanse of timber, Duff slowed the four-horse team. And as soon as the level of noise had fallen enough so talk was possible without need to raise his voice much above normal, Ruben showed a warm smile, said:

'I'm Ruben Bannin', mister. Guy you give a hand to is Eugene Miller. That's Edward Duffy drivin' us. Richard Shelby's takin' care of Pete Race. Who you already know from sharin' the hospitality of the Munro jailhouse with him.'

The half-breed nodded just to Banning, replied: 'Edge. No first name anyone's used in a long time.'

'What is it you do in Munro?' Banning asked, smiling still as the wagon rolled into the dark moon shadows of the wood.

His voice was pleasant toned, a match for the expression, but in the dark Edge sensed all eyes gazed toward him with deep suspicion as the old-timers awaited his reply.

'I'm just a passing-through stranger in this part of the country, feller.'

'If that's so!' Shelby blurted, obviously eager to make the point ahead of the others he guessed had it in mind to ask the same question, 'how come you were puttin' cash in the town bank?'

Edge supplied evenly: 'To pay off a debt, feller.'

'Oh, yeah?' Shelby again, triumph mixed with contempt when he was certain he caught out Edge in a lie. 'A stranger in town and you got debts there?'

The half-breed said: 'Don't as a rule talk about my private business with outsiders. But I'm making an exception in this case.'

'Real wise of you to do that,' Miller advised, his tone menacing.

Even in the near pitch darkness of the timber, Edge made the conscious effort to keep his face impassive: which helped prevent any hint of taut anger sounding in his voice as he responded evenly: 'A lady in Cheyenne loaned me the money. Happen to know there's a branch of the Western States Bank in Cheyenne. That other lady you held up in Munro this afternoon told me it was possible to have the hundred and——'

'That's fine, just fine, Mr Edge,' Banning cut in. 'You don't have to go into all the details. Like you say, it's none of our business.'

'Which is robbing banks,' Edge said wryly.

'Not only banks,' Banning replied, unruffled, added: 'And not any more, usually.'

Shelby muttered irritably: 'What if it's part of his business to break outta jail with Pete. Hired on to pretend he's what he ain't so he can——'

'He didn't volunteer to help!' Miller snapped. 'And——'

'And, anyway,' Banning interjected, reclaimed the focus of attention in the darkness. 'A guy that was planted to do what you say, Rich: I don't figure he'd stand by and let a kid get gunned down without tryin' to do somethin' to stop it.'

'He was——' Miller attempted to make an additional point.

'And, anyway, again,' Banning pressed on. 'How could they know we'd take steps to get Pete outta there? No, Rich, you are clutchin' at straws in your eagerness to find substance for unfounded suspicion.'

In the darkness it was suddenly clear Ruben Banning was not the ill-educated, unsophisticated good old boy he most of the time pretended to be.

'Damn right!' Miller agreed, concerned to justify his decision to ask the stranger for help. 'Like I was gonna say, Edge was in jail because they figured he's one of us.'

Shelby vented a scornful grunt.

'Yeah, I can see how that could be,' Banning allowed pensively. 'The way he had the woman at the bank open up the safe just about when we walked in.'

'And I can tell you guys somethin' else!' Miller announced. 'Edge was thinkin' about goin' his own way. Maybe he would've done it, and to hell with his gun and hundred and fifty bucks, if I'd give him half a chance. He'd have ditched Pete and took off.'

Although he could not see the man's face, Edge was sure

55

from his tone of voice Miller was not acting wise after the event. He was letting Edge know that, old and near-sighted as he was, he had indeed spotted signs that made him realise the half-breed would have reneged on their deal if the circumstances had suited him.

Edge said: 'I figured you were watching real close, feller.'

Talk lapsed for awhile as Duffy continued to hold the heavily breathing horses to an easy walk on the trail that twisted and turned through the timber: took the line of least resistance among the trees, the easiest route to avoid knolls and skirt hollows. So there were few grades, and these were only slight.

In the stillness of the wood that normally would be disturbed only by the unobtrusive sounds of secretive wildlife, tonight alarmed into silence by the intrusion of the wagon, Edge became uncomfortably aware of just how cold was the Colorado night. After the tensions and excitements of the jailbreak when the risk of getting shot, maybe killed, had generated its own inner, quick-to-cool heat.

He moved into a more comfortable position, his back against the rear of the box seat where Duffy sat. Turned up the collar of the sheepskin coat. Resisted the temptation to push his hands deep into the pockets. Felt that among this bunch of strange, unpredictable, old men it was wiser to have cold hands that were free. In the event if should be necessary to counter an unexpected move against him: to make him a more secure prisoner than he already was. Or worse.

He heard scrabbling noises in the darkness and when the meandering trail ran clear of the timber he saw the rest of the men on the rear of the wagon had also gotten themselves more comfortable and hunkered down into their coats. They had also taken steps to stress Edge was only among them on their terms.

Banning, Shelby and Miller all sat with rifles resting across their legs. And now they were able to see what they were doing in the clear moonlight, Banning and Shelby drew their revolvers, began to eject spent cartridge cases, feed fresh shells into the chambers.

Without a word being spoken, or a look exchanged,

Eugene Miller—who had fired just the one killing shot from his Colt—sat with his hand negligently draped over the frame of his Winchester while the others reloaded their handguns.

Then Duffy chose the right moment to glance down over his shoulder into the rear of the wagon. Saw the men were ready before he commanded the team into another spurt.

But no longer on the trail that directly ahead cut down into a small canyon. Instead he veered the rig into a sharp turn to the south that forced everyone to reach out, hold on tight.

Miller and Shelby roared harsh curses at the suddenness of the swing to the left, then more as the wheels juddered over rugged ground.

Banning seemed to bite back on an angry response, but his glowering expression matched those of the other two furious men.

The breakneck speed lasted for a couple of hundred yards or so. Before Duffy responded to the curses hurled at him from behind. Eased up on the frenzied pace, turned with a broad grin that revealed two wide gaps in his teeth.

The cursing died down.

'All right, all right,' the driver growled, displaced the grin with a scowl. 'But you guys are all the time gettin' to prove how good you are with sixshooters and rifles. You said for me to make time, Rube, whenever I reckoned could do it. And I know I can make it across this lousy piece of country without wreckin' the rig!'

While three old men continued to glare bitterly at the fourth, like young children locked in a battle of wills over an unimportant issue, Edge peered behind the wagon. Saw what his bruised rear end already knew about the kind of terrain they had crossed since Duffy turned off the trail. It was rough: the kind of ground that required a highly skilled teamster to drive a rig across it at dangerous high speed.

'We know it, Duff!' Banning said hurriedly, soothingly. Before either the scowling Shelby or Miller could take outraged issue with the driver. 'Any time we need to make fast time over the worst kinda country, you're the guy for the job.'

He was in his good old boy guise again. Now was like a full

grown adult, soothing the ruffled feelings of a child.

'But there ain't no posse breathin' down our necks yet!' Shelby snarled.

'That's right,' Banning agreed. 'And now we're off the trail, you can take it pretty easy gettin' us to Eagle Rock, uh?' He gestured toward Race. 'For his sake, Duff?'

'Sure,' Duffy allowed, petulantly pacified.

'Sure!' Shelby echoed sullenly. 'And Pete's lookin' and soundin' worse every minute. Could be even he won't make it home.'

Miller complained: 'Don't be such a damn old pessimist, Rich! Pete's the toughest of all us old coots, is my opinion.'

'Until he took that bullet in the ribs and fell off his horse!' Duffy countered, grunted irritably and faced front again. Gave his full attention to steering the team at a sedate pace across the broken ground littered with scattered boulders, deep hollows and an obstacle course of thorny brush and stunted trees.

During another silence that lasted several minutes, concern for their wounded partner started to give way to renewed mistrust of Edge. Banning sensed the tension-charged situation coming to a head, spoke before the frowning Shelby could voice a barbed comment.

'In his day, which ain't entirely over yet, Duff's driven every kinda vehicle over all kinds of country, Edge.'

The half-breed inclined his head slightly, took out the makings.

'We're all of us tradesmen of one sort or another,' Banning went on. His attitude seemed preoccupied, like his mind was concerned with a subject of far greater importance than the one he had elected to raise. 'Apart from stealin' from those who are well able to carry the losses, you understand?'

Edge gave another almost imperceptible nod as he began to roll a cigarette.

'Pete used to be a seaman on a whaler out of 'Frisco. Gene, he hunted buffalo in the old days.'

Miller augmented: 'Before my eyes went bad on me and I couldn't see worth a damn much more than past the muzzle of the rifle.' He spat forcefully off the side of the wagon. 'But the buffalo had just about been hunted out by then, anyways.'

'Rich Shelby, he's still a saloonkeeper and——'

'What you tellin' him all this stuff for, Rube?' Shelby demanded irritably.

Banning replied with a shrug: 'The man was open enough to tell us some of his private business. With time to kill, there's no harm in a little conversation about days gone by. Anyway, want Edge to know we ain't just your average, ordinary, run-of-the-mill bunch of desperadoes stealin' other folks money for personal gain. What you called us, right? A bunch of desperadoes?'

He looked long and hard at Edge as he appeared to relish the phrase, like it had a discernible taste he enjoyed. 'No, sir... We got us a fine cause to work toward these days.'

'And what that is sure ain't nobody's business but our own!'

It was Eugene Miller who made this point with such force. And Shelby and Duffy glared at Banning: challenged him to continue with this line of talk at his peril.

No longer preoccupied, and not looking like an uncle now, Banning seemed about to respond with fury to the minor insurrection against his authority. Then the forces ranged against him, or his own good sense in realising they were right, acted to drain him of tension. He waved a dismissive hand, allowed:

'You guys think I'm stupid or somethin'? Mile of difference between passin' the time of day and passin' on just why we do what we do. Why we had good reason to hit the Munro bank today and——'

'Rube, quit it!' Miller snarled. And not for the first time his attitude suggested the bespectacled old-timer was number two in the chain of command among the group.

Banning nodded and shrugged. And this signalled another silence on the rear of the wagon as it constantly swung left and right, Duffy skilfully picking the way among the obstacles that gave the smoothest ride: generally heading ultimately toward the south west, Edge judged.

In this time the old men were withdrawn deep into private worlds of frowning thought from which Edge seemed to be excluded. But there was nothing to be gained from this. For although they were old and preoccupied and some of them were infirm, they were also armed and they outnumbered him.

Anyway, out here in the middle of nowhere there was little point in attempting to escape: if he was, indeed, a prisoner? Except for verbal abuse from the naturally aggressive Rich Shelby and how Edward Duffy made no secret he mistrusted him, Edge had been well treated since he was hauled aboard the wagon. There had been no harm done him, nor any attempt made to shackle him.

So he was content to maintain the *status quo*. For now. Maybe the deal would be honoured by the old-timers when they reached Eagle Rock: he would get his gun and his money back. Which would leave him short just his horse and gear: plus he would still be wanted for having a hand in the murder of young Nick Cornwall at the Munro jailhouse.

He pinched the glow out of the butt of the cigarette and tossed it off the side of the wagon: briefly considered the priorities once he had gotten back what these old-timers who robbed for a good reason had taken from him.

First he needed to get at least one of them back to Munro: to prove his innocence of complicity in the robbery and killing. Next settle the debt owed Nancy Raven. Finally recommence his trip to California.

But it was futile to consider yet just how to achieve what had to be done. For it seemed clear they were headed for the place where they left the horses they rode into town for the bank raid. Along with their ill-gotten gains from the bank? Once there—at Eagle Rock?—he could think about his next move. In the meantime, best he just waited and watched for any surprises the old-timers might spring on him. Certain, at least, he was not going to be gunned down in cold blood.

Maybe?

'Hey!' Banning exclaimed. 'I didn't get through tellin' you as much as I'm allowed about us, did I?'

He glowered at the startled Shelby and Miller, and at the suddenly rigid back of Duffy. And again Edge was aware of the juvenile level of relationship that became established

60

among the bunch of old men in certain circumstances: invariably when they had cause to disagree or to be jealous of each other. And the term 'second childhood' flicked through his mind as he told Banning:

'I'm not much interested in anything about any of you: except you have a gun and a hundred and fifty dollars of mine.'

Banning revealed his quickness of temper as he switched the hot-eyed glare from his partners to the half-breed, warned grimly: 'I'm still considerin' if I'll go along with that deal Gene made with you!'

Edge answered evenly with a shrug: 'I'm in no shape to be in a hurry for a decision, feller.'

'Keep that in mind,' Banning growled, his irritation diminishing.

'Keep it in mind you ain't in no shape to ask for nothin'!' Shelby snarled to align himself firmly with Banning's threat of no deal.

Duffy grunted, presumably in agreement with this. And Miller wriggled self-consciously when Edge said:

'Someone in a group makes a deal, I figure it ought to be honoured by the rest.'

'That's a good rule of thumb, mister,' Banning allowed with a sage nod that gave the impression he had carefully considered the point on many previous occasions. 'But our group isn't like a lot of others. We're different. Got different rules.'

Edge nodded. 'I'd noticed.'

Banning smiled, like he chose to accept the comment as a compliment. 'And not just because we're all a little long in the tooth and stiff in the joints to do what we do.'

'Right. You've got high ideals, too.'

'That's a long story I'm not goin' to get into again, mister!' His tone was abruptly hard and an accompanying glower was directed at Shelby, Miller and Duffy: who this time twisted his head around, joined in issuing the tacit warning. Then Banning looked again at Edge, reached his point. 'No, I never got to tell you what I used to do before I lost the leg and had to give it up.' He rapped on his wooden limb with the barrel of the Winchester. 'I was a major in the United States Army, mister. And this fine body of men all served under me. Saw a lot of action together, didn't we guys?'

'Sure did, Rube,' Eugene Miller said eagerly.

Richard Shelby came close to smiling at faded memories as he agreed: 'No arguin' with that, good buddies.'

Without turning around, Edward Duffy mused: 'Sure ain't. All kinds of action, in a whole lot of different places.'

Banning gazed into the middle distance where perhaps he saw vivid images of long ago, said reflectively: 'War and peace.'

Into the new easy silence that the talk of the past had heralded, Edge murmured: 'Which is another long story.'

7

For over an hour they rode without talking through the cold night across the plateau of broken ground surrounded by the distant rugged ridges of the Rockies. Duffy giving the impression he knew exactly where he was going: the others obviously having as much confidence in his navigational skills as his driving ability.

Sometimes somebody spat off the side. Occasionally a set joint cracked. Edge smoked two cigarettes.

They had been on another trail, heading due west, for something over two miles, when Duffy announced:

'The Eagle Rock fork's up ahead, you guys.'

These, the first words spoken for a long time, caused everyone on the rear of the wagon to jerk free of the thoughts that occupied him. Even, it seemed, the unconscious Pete Race reacted to the news. Certainly he uttered a low groan: that held mental anguish rather than physical pain.

Eugene Miller was dozing at the time, if the frightened grunt and then the embarrassed look he directed about himself were signs of how far his mind had wandered as the wagon made its slow, smooth progress.

Edge rose to his feet with the others, and all of them braced themselves against the back of the seat, to peer ahead. And over a distance of a half mile or so the half-breed saw why the granite monolith that towered some fifty feet into the air at a fork in the trail was called Eagle Rock. Certainly from this direction, now that moonlight bathed the outcrop, it bore a strong resemblance to an eagle's head sculptured by the elements. There was even a hole, or maybe a patch of lighter coloured rock, close to the top that looked like the gleaming eye of a gigantic bird perched up there.

For a few moments Edge sensed the deep relief that gripped

the men as they surveyed their next objective since they successfully broke Pete Race out of the Munro jailhouse: shattered when Duffy suddenly craned his head forward, a joint in his spine cracking, groaned:

'Oh, shit, it looks like there's somebody there! You guys see that?'

Even more than before, mass attention was concentrated on the point ahead where one fork of the trail continued to run westward across the plateau, the other angled to the south west. But even as Edge heard a rifle hammer thumbed back, saw the other two men standing alongside him take firmer grips on their repeaters, he knew he was not being totally ignored.

Anyway, it was not yet time for him to make his move against the tense old-timers. He kept fresh in his mind the way how, in the middle of a town, Eugene Miller had not hesitated to fire a killing shot at a kid he mistakenly thought was trying to reach for a gun. So out here, merely suspecting somebody was hidden at an isolated spot a half mile distant, none of the old-timers would hesitate to violently rid themselves of a distraction.

The short-sighted Miller blurted anxiously: 'What? I don't see nothin' to show that there's——'

'Yeah, there's a wagon right alongside the cabin, Gene,' Banning explained.

It was Shelby who had cocked the hammer of his Winchester. He now raised the rifle and aimed it from his shoulder, crouched down so he could steady the barrel across the seat backrest alongside Duffy.

'And I'm pretty damn sure I saw a flicker of light, Rube,' Duffy rasped. 'Folks restin' up for the night, they don't usually need a light at this time, uh? Guess it's gotta be way after midnight, you figure?'

'Don't you go firin' before there's real need of it, Rich,' Banning instructed, waited until the belligerent man with the levelled rifle responded with a disgruntled sound, then added icily: 'I ain't never heard of a posse travellin' by wagon.'

There was an interruption to the talk that lasted maybe fifteen seconds while the distance between the slow-moving wagon and the strangely eroded outcrop narrowed by as many feet. Then Duffy asked thickly:

'You want me to keep her rollin', Rube?'

'Sure thing.'

There was no vocal response from anybody. Just a spontaneous intake of breath. This was held as the men prepared themselves to face up to a possible danger they had not counted on. And in this tense atmosphere the turning of wheels, the setting down of hooves, the creaking of timbers seemed suddenly much louder.

The laboured breathing of Pete Race, too, sounded inordinately loud.

Edge was as tense in his own way as everyone else while he fixed his narrowed-eyed gaze on the rock in the fork of the trail. Where a wagon that looked like a Conestoga was parked near its base and what he thought was a heap of rocks between the covered rig and the outcrop, and now realised were the remains of a building: no more than a roofless, three-walled shell.

Against the darkness, a light flared.

Shelby uttered a strangled cry of alarm, Miller brought his rifle to the aim, rested it on the seat backrest at the other side of Duffy from Shelby as the driver hauled on the reins with a curse.

Banning rasped: 'Easy, you guys.'

A match had been struck: a second match if Duffy had seen a flicker of light earlier. It was touched to the oil-sodden wick of a lamp, and the next moment the interior of the three-walled remains of a building was filled with yellow light.

The lamp was raised high by a man in a dark suit. In his other hand something glinted metallically in the light.

'Shit, that a gun he's got?' Eugene Miller wanted to know, his voice croakier than ever with apprehension as he craned anxiously forward when the wagon jolted to a halt.

The team snorted their relief at being rested.

Edge said: 'No, feller. Looks like a brass telescope.'

Banning had started to bring up his rifle. Now let the stock drop to the wagon bed with a thud, scoffed: 'Stands to reason it wouldn't be a gun, Gene. The guy's not gonna light a lamp and show himself an easy target if he figured to shoot at us.'

The man dropped the telescope in a side pocket of his suit jacket, beckoned to signal that the wagon should come forward.

'Go ahead, Duff,' Banning instructed.

'You sure, Rube?' Shelby growled thickly.

'Sure I'm sure, damnit!' The sudden flash of temper demonstrated the degree of strain Banning was under. As Duffy started the wagon rolling, he controlled his tone to tell the half-breed: 'And a word to the guy who's been a wise one up to now?'

Edge looked quizzically at the leader of the bunch.

'Don't have no idea how much store you set by human life? But you better know that if you do or say anythin' tricky while we're findin' out what's what here, it won't be just your neck on the line? I guess you understand me?'

'I set about as much store by it as you fellers do.'

Miller muttered defensively: 'Hell, I never planned to kill that kid at the Munro law office. It was just lousy luck the bullet took him in his stupid head.'

'Blood under the bridge,' Edge answered. 'And Cornwall wasn't anything to you. The way your buddy hasn't been breathing for the past couple of minutes, that should've given you a little grief.'

There was a stretched second of tense silence. Then Banning rasped:

'Keep her movin', Duff!'

'Shit... Pete!' Shelby gasped. And he ignored the man in the lamplight at the derelict building between the outcrop and the Conestoga, dropped to his haunches beside Race and bent his head low to listen for his breathing.

'Rich?' Miller asked anxiously.

'He's right, Goddamnit! Pete's gone! Oh, my God, his clothes are soakin'!' He displayed a darkly stained hand. 'Poor bastard must have plain bled to death!'

'Welcome to you!' the man holding the lamp yelled, shattered the silence that greeted Shelby's bad news, his voice loud and clear against the muted, duller sounds of the wagon. 'Unless this is your property, perhaps? And I am the intruder?'

Edge thought it was the kind of voice that was often raised: to address listeners over a great distance, or perhaps a large audience. Not just the tone, but the choice of words pointed to an actor, or a preacher maybe.

'Damnit, Ruben!' Shelby blurted. There was a catch in his voice, like he was close to spilling tears over his newly dead partner. He needed to swallow hard before he could go on: 'It's just like what happened to Charlie in that——'

'Quit that kinda talk!' Miller rasped.

'Yeah, save it, Rich!' Duffy snapped. 'What'll we do, Rube?'

'We'll play along with him,' Banning said evenly. 'Act nice and friendly. Unless things get altered by outside influences.'

There was a query in his tone, addressed to Edge. The half-breed said:

'Right now I'm still just interested in my gun and hundred and fifty bucks, feller.'

Duffy spat between the rumps of the horses, growled sourly: 'He's like the damn parrot an old aunt of mine had once. Way he keeps on sayin' the same damn thing over and over.'

'Shut up!' Banning snapped.

'Did you hear what I said?' the man called. 'I am Conrad Christie and if I am trespassing, it was not my intention to do so. If you are travellers, like I, you are welcome to share this night camp.'

'Here!' Banning said to Edge.

There was a shocked gasp from Shelby as he rose from beside the corpse of Race. Then a similar reaction from Miller who had sensed something amiss and snapped his head around.

Edge said: 'It'll do for now. I'm much obliged.'

Banning had drawn his Colt, now held it loosely around the outside of the trigger guard and the cylinder, offered it butt-first to Edge as he said: 'A sign of good faith?'

'Deal,' Edge replied and slid the revolver into his own holster.

'Crazy,' Shelby murmured.

Before Miller had time to voice an opinion, Christie spoke first.

'I said——' he started, apprehension sounding in his voice, the trembling of his hand seen as the lamp shook.

'No sweat, Christie!' Edge broke in on him. 'Be glad to accept your hospitality.'

There was now only a couple of hundred yards between the wagon and the brightly lit area at the base of the outcrop which did not resemble anything from this close: it was just a tower of hard and unyielding grey rock.

'Who the frig do you think you are?' Shelby snapped. 'You don't speak for us!'

Edge shrugged. 'So do your own talking to the feller. When you're through acting dumb.'

'What?' Shelby looked like he was about to swing his rifle toward Edge.

'Damnit, Rich!' Banning snarled. 'He's right. We've been actin' like we're dumb and that sure ain't smart.' He raised his voice, the false easiness of his tone probably not sounding over a distance. 'Edge is right, Mr Christie. Like he says, there's nothin' to worry about. They're our horses you must've found out back of that there old way station. But we don't have property rights here. Be real happy to spend a little time with you before we move on by.'

'Just like a friggin' church picnic,' Shelby growled scornfully.

'Yeah, just like that,' Banning rasped at the sour-tempered man. 'Guy looks and sounds like he could be a minister, even. So no cussin', spittin', breakin' wind or talkin' dirty in front of him.' He looked from Shelby to Miller, then at Edge. 'Everyone agree to that? For the sake of that real friendly-soundin' guy up ahead?'

The wagon had rolled into the circle of light from the lamp. And when Duffy reined the team to a halt there was not time nor opportunity for replies.

Christie greeted: 'Good evening, gentlemen. Yes, I saw the horses, of course. Wondered about them, naturally. I would have pressed on to find another night camp had I not been so deeply tired from travel.'

Christie was in his mid thirties. A tall, rangy, long-faced man with sandy hair, deepset dark eyes, a Roman nose and wide, thin-lipped mouth. His three piece suit and bootlace tie were black, his shirt white. The clothing was old but well cared for.

There was still some tension in back of his smile but he did not look afraid as he put down the lamp. Although he had a compulsion to continue talking as he watched the four old-timers and Edge climb down off the wagon.

'I'm a schoolteacher. From Pennsylvania, bound for California and a new life of peace and happiness, I hope.'

'Fine aims, sir,' Ruben Banning said as he hobbled forward. He leaned heavily on his cane, more so than Edge recalled from the bank robbery and he wondered if the avuncular looking man with the beaming face under the horseshoe of grey hair was playing up his infirmity to gain some sympathy that might pay off later.

Then he saw the other three old men, most noticeably the stiff-legged Rich Shelby, were also walking with pained awkwardness. And next became aware of his own dis-comforts as he moved for the first time after hours of riding on the wagon that had shuddered and shaken all of them despite Duffy's skilled driving.

'To get to the golden state of California and to seek peace and happiness there,' the old man with the stick went on. 'Many have sought this and I wish you much luck in succeedin'.'

The final heeltaps of tension drained out of Conrad Christie as he listened to Ruben Banning's words, saw his amiable smile. Then he responded eagerly as Banning, his right hand occupied with the cane, held out his left to offer a warm clasp of greeting.

Christie came forward, extended his right hand, laughed as the left hand of the other man required he turn his wrist to complete the unorthodox clasp.

'Now, guys,' Banning said. Not loud, but with latent power in his tone. Snatched the cane off the ground, jerked at the hand of the younger, fitter man. Next swept the cane through an arc that cracked it viciously into the side of Christie's left knee. Exploded a cry of agony from him as he was plunged forcefully forward, went full length to the ground.

Banning, fully prepared for the changing momentum, was able to splay his good leg away from the wooden limb, remain evenly balanced.

His partners were prepared for something unexpected to happen. Obviously knew from past experience how to respond. Had their revolvers drawn and aimed down at Christie before he hit the ground.

Edge was one of a line of four men in back of Banning: Shelby to his right, Duffy and Miller to the left. Knew in one split second of intense thought that his life depended upon the decision he made in the next split second. That if he allowed his hand instinctively to draw Banning's revolver, there would be a bloodbath. From which he might escape... If he gunned down the four old-timers... Who, if they did not kill him, would surely kill Conrad Christie.

He made the decision: held absolutely still. Tore his gaze away from Banning who now pressed the tip of his cane into Christie's neck. Flicked his eyes to the right, then left as the hammers of the three Colts were thumbed back.

'You made the wise choice, Mr Edge,' Banning said without turning. 'If we all keep actin' wisely, no one'll get hurt the least little bit.'

'This is stupid!' Christie gasped, not moving a muscle as the cane remained digging into the side of his neck. 'All I wanted was to be friendly to strangers on the trail.'

'The stupidity is all yours, Mr Christie,' Banning argued evenly, now removed the cane, used it to support himself as he moved a few paces to the side.

Christie looked up at him, received a nod of approval and rose on to all fours, rested, was shaken by a dry retch then clambered unsteadily to his feet. His unfolding form was cautiously tracked by the three revolvers in the rock-steady grips of the old-timers.

'These men and I did not reach such venerable ages by being stupid, young man.' Banning was letting his education show again, choosing and enunciating his words carefully. 'I of course discount the gentleman who has not drawn his side arm. Like you, he was foolish enough to allow himself to become involved with the meanest bunch of desperadoes who

70

ever rode this piece of Godforsaken country.'

He was suddenly less well spoken as he once again relished the term Edge had applied to the old-timers.

'What are you going to do?' Christie asked as his fingertips explored the side of his neck where the tarnished ferrule of Banning's cane had dug in.

Edge sensed the men in the line with him were starting to tire of the man's rhetoric as he echoed:

'What are we going to do? We are going to continue to pursue those same aims that brought you all the way out here from Pennsylvania. Peace and happiness, Mr Christie. If we can do that without killing anybody, that will be just fine and dandy. On the other hand, if it emerges that we cannot, well . . .'

Banning was content to leave the rest unspoken, satisfied the apprehensive schoolteacher could fill in the missing threat himself. But Shelby snarled:

'We kill people easy as we kill time, mister!' He directed a sidelong glance at Edge, showed a grim smile as he urged: 'Tell them, why don't you?'

'Speaking of time,' Edge said, briefly met Shelby's smile with an icy grin, then swept his gaze to a glassless window in the wall of the building shell to the right.

The woman he had glimpsed aiming a rifle through the window a moment ago said evenly: 'I'd advise you three old farts to drop your guns, or your time'll be up.'

Edge murmured to complete what he had been saying: 'Seems the watch has stopped.'

8

Ruben Banning raked his suddenly-tired gaze from the woman at the hole in the wall to the line of men behind him. Then he looked at Christie, who gave him a sharp nod.

He instructed his partners: 'Do like the lady says, boys.'

'I don't think——' Shelby started.

'You hardly ever do, Rich,' Duffy groaned, tossed his revolver to the ground six feet in front of him. 'Just do like Rube tells you, you crazy old coot!'

Miller ditched his Colt in the same area, looking sick to his stomach. And two tense seconds later Shelby did likewise, sullenly muttering something about the woman being no lady and this being no church picnic.

'Excellent,' Conrad Christie said, took a wide detour around Banning, stooped to gather up the Colts and pushed one in the pocket opposite to that where the telescope was stowed, held the others one in each hand. 'I should warn you that Alice, my wife, is quite some markswoman with a Winchester repeating rifle over a considerably longer range than this.'

Alice withdrew from the window, emerged into full view at the crumbled end of the wall that had once formed a front corner of the way station.

A head shorter than her husband, she had a plain face: round with a button nose and small eyes. Her hair was mouse brown and hung in bangs to her eyebrows. Her freckled skin was pitted with the scars of old acne. She was at least ten years younger than her husband and the smile she now spread across her homely face would perhaps have been tomboyish in normal circumstances. But in the tense situation that existed tonight it held an evil quality which if it owed anything to humour was of the graveyard kind.

She wore a shapeless grey dress of homespun fabric that showed she was no lightweight: hinted she was maybe pregnant.

'You sure about Edge?' she asked of Banning. Then there was in the way she studied the half-breed a strong suggestion she was sure of something about him: he had the kind of looks she liked.

'He's not one of us,' Banning confirmed wearily, genuine fatigue in his voice. The way he stood, leaning heavily on his cane, and the haggard look on his round face likewise conveyed this was all too much for him after a long, wearing day. The spirit that had kept him perky while things went right had fast drained out of him now they had gone badly awry.

'I'll do you some kind of harm if you aim any of those guns at me without the intention of shooting me,' Edge said, suddenly deeply tired himself as he stepped out of the line, swung to pass in front of Duffy and Miller. This took him away from the woman with the rifle. And he backed off from the man with a revolver in each hand.

'He gives people just the one warnin',' Banning augmented, rubbing his tired eyes.

'He don't say a lot,' Shelby sneered and weariness diluted the scorn in his tone.

'Except about himself,' Duffy added. 'And mostly repeats it all the time, like a parrot my Aunt Rosina once had.'

'This all seems unreal,' Miller said huskily, and shifted his bespectacled gaze constantly around everyone standing in the circle of yellow light from the lamp on the ground. 'It was all goin' so well and now Pete's——'

Alice Christie vented a sound between a howl of anger and a cry of dismay. It cut off what Eugene Miller was saying, focused all attention on her as she swung to the side, dropped into a half crouch, rifle aimed at the rear of the wagon.

'Alice?' her husband croaked, his newfound composure shattered.

'There's another of them, Con! Still on their wagon!'

'He's dead, ma'am,' Edge supplied as he took out the makings.

73

'Shit,' Alice rasped, her cheeks ballooned. Then she shook her head, straightened up, asked: 'What now, Con?'

'Edge, that your name?' Christie said.

The half-breed had started to roll a cigarette as he looked carefully around at his surroundings for the first time since he peered at the area over a narrowing distance when Duffy called attention to the nearness of Eagle Rock.

Saw that the Conestoga parked beyond the wall where the woman appeared was much like the couple who had ridden it all the way from Pennsylvania to the Rockies. It had a lot of rough mileage in back of it, but if it had ever been allowed to fall into disrepair, it had been carefully restored with scant concern for good looks.

Unlike the stage line way station that had not been used for its original purpose in a very long time. Now consisted only of the three crumbling walls, the highest at the back windowless and the two side walls each with a hole for a window. Whatever timber had been used in the frames, the door that had evidently been in the missing front wall, and the roof, had long since been removed, or rotted, maybe been used to fuel the number of fires travellers had lit within the wreckage of the former building.

There was no smell in the chill night air of recent burning, so it was probable the most recent pile of grey and black ashes were the remains of a cooking fire the bunch of aged desperadoes had lit on their first or second visit here today—yesterday, if it was after midnight. When they first got here with the wagon and saddle horses, switched from one to the other for the bank raid. Or when they returned, a man short. To rest up and plan the jailbreak.

But what did it matter? The homely Alice Christie was right. Now was of consequence. The past only mattered in terms of how what happened now cleared up the doubts left by it.

'That's my name, feller,' the half-breed answered, struck a match on the jutting butt of Banning's revolver, lit the cigarette.

'This is unreal to us, too. Totally outside our usual experience. I'd certainly appreciate it if you'd explain how

74

this extremely unnerving situation came about?'

Edge nodded. 'The five old-timers robbed the branch of the Western States Bank in a town called Munro, few miles north east of here. Way it happened, I got caught up in the robbery and Munro people figured I was part of it. They locked me up with him.'

He jerked a thumb toward the wagon where Alice had seen the inert form of Race.

'He was still alive then, but he was unconscious. Couldn't tell anyone I didn't have a hand in the robbery. The rest of these fellers came back to town to bust him out of the jailhouse. A deputy was killed and the way that looked, I was part of it, too. Figured it best to string along. Wait for a chance to get clear. Is this it?'

Christie ignored the direct question, countered with a query of his own. 'The horses that Alice and I found here some hours ago? Long before I saw you people coming down the road on the wagon?'

He kept one gun aimed as he patted the pocket in which the telescope rested.

Edge told him with a shrug: 'I'd just be guessing, feller?'

Shelby cleared his throat and scowled, like he was about to snarl an obscenity.

Banning said lethargically: 'Me and my boys ain't so young as we used to be, young man. We find it kinder on our ancient bones to ride a wagon than horseback. But you can't hit a bank and make a fast getaway aboard a wagon. Thus the horses. We used the wagon for the second trip to Munro because we didn't know how badly poor Pete Race was injured.'

'Bad as it can get!' Shelby said, and spat on the ground just in front of his boots.

'Same question,' Alice said. 'What now, Con?'

Edge spared the time on the inconsequential thought that the woman came from further east than Pennsylvania. He guessed New York: not uptown.

Christie seemed indecisive: obviously a state he was unused to. While his wife continued to be patiently receptive to whatever was asked of her.

Edge wondered if any of the old-timers shared his view of the situation: that if something tripped a panic switch in Christie's mind, his wife would be perfectly willing to follow whatever instruction or example he gave her.

Which bothered him, since he needed at least one of the old-timers coherently alive to prove himself innocent of the Munro bank robbery and murder.

It was Miller who blurted: 'Damnit, Ruben, we could all of us wind up dead unless somethin'——'

'These fellers stole a hundred and fifty bucks of mine from the bank,' Edge cut in. 'This Colt I'm packing is only on free loan until I'm given back my own.'

'Just like my old aunt's friggin' parrot, didn't I tell you?' Duffy muttered irritably.

Christie suddenly reached a decision, announced: 'This is none of our business, Alice. We'll send them on their way, then be on ours.'

She nodded, acknowledged flatly: 'Whatever you say, Con.'

'I guess we don't have any objection to that.' A glimmer of Banning's former perkiness had returned.

Edge growled: 'He's not speaking for me, Christie.'

'I'm afraid I'm not able to help you too much right now, Mr Edge.' He sounded and looked like he truly did regret it. 'But I can offer you a choice: to remain here after they leave and pursue your own ends thereafter: or to go with them. Should you elect to go with them, I must insist you leave the revolver here.'

Edge looked from the nervous Christie to the suddenly tense Alice: was sure he could draw and gun down both of them with little risk of taking a well placed rifle shot or a stray revolver bullet. He asked of Banning:

'Where's my gun and the money?'

'The sonofabitch has sure got gall,' Duffy muttered.

Shelby spat a stream of saliva at the ground.

'Just one hundred and fifty bucks was the deal?' Banning reminded.

'Plus the gun.'

'Don't friggin' trust him, Rube!' Shelby warned sourly.

76

Edge pressed: 'Your end in return for me lending Miller a hand at the jailhouse.'

Banning looked long and hard at Edge, like he was trying to penetrate the mask of impassivity, read what was running through the mind of the man of few words, fewer expressions.

'Con, honey?' Alice Christie said softly.

'Alice?' He was still nervous, now perplexed.

'We're lettin' this get away from us, sweetheart.'

'I don't——'

'We're the people with the guns, Con.' She raised her voice just a little, hardened her mouthline a lot. 'Yet Edge and the old farts are wheelin' and dealin' like we ain't even here.'

Banning showed her a vexed frown as he reminded: 'Your husband admitted it was none of your business, young lady.'

The woman swung the rifle, triggered a shot that proved the claim she was an expert with a Winchester was not false. The bullet struck Banning's cane, blasted the bottom three inches off it.

As much from shock as the explosive lack of support, the one legged man fell heavily to the ground. Would have sprawled out, spreadeagled on his back, if he had not used the truncated cane to stay in a sitting position.

'Alice!' Christie's tone was shrill with censure.

'You know what I think, you old fart?' the woman said to Banning as she pumped the lever action of the repeater, the ejected shellcase glinted in the yellow light as it spun through the air, then pinged against the top of the lamp. 'I think you oldsters and this guy Edge are tryin' to give me and Con the business. Bunch of hardassed Westerners, figure you can put stuff across us greenhorn Easterners?'

She vented an unfeminine snort, then sneered: 'Fat friggin' chance!'

'Young lady, you should not mistreat the old and infirm. Some day you might reach a time when——'

'Don't you lecture me, Grandpa!' Alice broke in. 'Just get up on your feet. Or crawl. Or do whatever you gotta do so you and the rest—Edge if he's a mind—can get on that wagon and head on back to whatever rocks you slid out from under.'

'Young lady, I——'

'Guess I can be called young, but a lady I'm not! So quit with callin' me that!'

'That sure is right!' Shelby agreed grimly. 'A lady she ain't, Rube. But whatever the hell she is, I want to know about our horses and equipment before we leave like she wants. I can't afford to lose——'

'Con, go get them what they want.'

'You sure, Alice?'

She sighed, her temper cooling. Spared him a brief, loving glance, said: 'I've spent most of my life never bein' sure of nothin', honey. You know that. What you can be sure of right now: if you hear any shootin' while you're back there, be a bunch of dead old farts when you get back out here!'

Christie was held by more indecision for a few moments. Then he spun on his heels, went toward the front corner of the building across from where Alice stood.

Eugene Miller turned more slowly, started to amble toward the wagon. Duffy crouched beside Banning to help the struggling one-legged man to get up. Shelby seemed rigid with anger, like he did not trust himself to move in case it triggered him into some reckless act that might prove fatally stupid.

Edge dropped the part-smoked cigarette, ground it out under a heel, instructed evenly: 'Hold it, feller.'

All gazes went toward him, no one sure who he meant. Saw he was peering at the uneasy bespectacled man who had halted in mid-stride alongside the horses in the wagon traces.

'Now what's this about?' Alice demanded suspiciously.

Edge moved toward the wagon as Miller's fear gave way to anger which seemed to generate a palpable heat in the coldness of the fall night.

A tense silence would have enveloped the lamplighted area at the base of Eagle Rock had not some horses out back of the former way station made disgruntled sounds at being disturbed.

Then Edge added to the body of unobtrusive noise as he leaned over the rear of the wagon, next reached under the seat. He sensed many eyes fixed upon him, then heard the woman's sigh of relief, grunts of anger from some of the men as he backed off from the wagon. He held four Winchesters by the muzzle ends of their barrels, swung them up to rest across his left shoulder.

'A fine try, Gene,' Banning consoled bitterly.

'He's a sneaky sonofabitch, ain't he, Ruben?' Duffy complained as he gave Banning the shortened cane.

The one-legged man could support himself on this, albeit bent over a little. Duffy went on in the same whining tone:

'He don't forget nothin'. We never should've trusted him to——'

'Bein' wise after the event serves no purpose,' Banning cut in wearily. 'All we can do is learn from our mistakes, Duff.'

He executed a half bow toward the woman as her husband reappeared out of the shadows beyond the side wall into the pool of lamplight. Christie was leading a string of five horses.

Banning asked of Edge: 'I suppose in these circumstances you'll take more than your own money?'

Shelby snarled: 'And share it out with this couple——'

'Alice and I have been called many names,' Christie cut in. 'But whatever else we may actually be, we are honest. We have no intention of making financial gain out of this distressing incident!'

'So where's our saddles and other stuff then?' Shelby demanded, almost childishly petutant again.

'I just have the one pair of hands!' Christie snapped. And for the first time there was ill temper in his demeanour as he jerked on the reins to lead the horses to the rear of the wagon.

Where he did a double-take at Edge with the clutch of rifles rested on his shoulder. Said with a slow shake of his head: 'This gets weirder by the minute.'

'Even curiouser and curiouser?' the half-breed suggested with a low key-smile that altered his mouthline but did not touch his narrowed eyes.

'Is there an allusion in that I should understand?' the schoolteacher asked as he began to hitch the reins to the rear of the wagon.

Edge shook his head, drawled: 'Forget it, feller. Just be grateful you landed such a wonderful wife as Alice.'

9

While the final preparations were being made for the bunch of old-timers to leave the Eagle Rock way station, Edge began to feel himself caught up in the general sense of unreality.

Just to have gotten enmeshed with such a decrepit group of bank robbers was unlikely enough. And the way he got locked up in a small town jailhouse, then was busted out seemed pretty damn strange. In retrospect could have had a dreamlike quality, were it not that the killing of the kid deputy made it unequivocally real.

Now he was allowing himself to be extricated from the influence of the old-timers by a plain, maybe pregnant girl from the wrong side of the New York tracks and her much more upper crust schoolteacher husband...

Edge kept a firm grip on the reality of his situation by staying busy while Conrad Christie went back into the shadowed darkness again, returned with a pair of saddles hung with the usual western trail-riding accroutrements. Then went back to bring out two more: by which time Edge was through with the clutch of rifles.

One at a time had pumped their actions, until each magazine was empty and the ground at his feet was littered with unfired bullets.

The old-timers had watched this with expressions that varied from Banning's resignation to Shelby's hatred, and included Duffy's contempt and a kind of melancholy that could have been something more forceful from behind the light-reflecting lenses of Miller's glasses.

All four of them occasionally looked away from the half-breed: at the ground, toward Christie when he reappeared, up at the towering rock, at the lamp, the crumbled walls, the

Conestoga, each other, their own wagon. Never at the plain woman in the plain dress with the Winchester levelled at them from her right hip.

Her stance was easy, and on her freckled and acne-scarred face the expression softened gradually to a tomboyish smile: mischievous instead of malevolent as the time for departure drew near. She grew more confident by the moment. She had never been uneasy except when she saw Race on the back of the wagon, did not realise he was dead. Also, Edge decided, she was even starting to enjoy this situation she now had fully under control.

When Christie came back into the lamplit area with a fifth saddle—probably Race's because a rifle jutted out of the boot—the half-breed looked at Ruben Banning, said:

'Like Aunt Rosina's parrot again?'

Reluctance caused the one-legged man to leave a momentary pause, then he sighed and shrugged. 'In my saddlebags. They're the ones with R.B. worked on them.'

Edge tossed the empty Winchesters back aboard the wagon, began to delve into a saddlebag without checking for identifying initials.

'I said the ones with . . .' Banning started to protest, made to hobble forward on the shortened cane.

'You want to see again how damn good I am with this rifle, mister?' Alice swung the Winchester, aimed it directly at the crippled man. 'Only it won't be no fancy stick I'll shoot out from under you next time!'

Banning froze, met the glare of the woman with a higher degree of smouldering anger than she directed at him.

Christie slid the rifle from the boot, pitched it aboard, told Edge: 'I already unloaded this one.'

Banning let the heat flow out of him on a sigh.

Edge said: 'Fine, feller. You want to check over some of these saddlebags with me? You know by now what interests me most. But look for extra shells, maybe extra guns at the same time.'

Now Banning vented a scornful snort. 'I only said me and the boys used to be in the United States Army, Edge! Didn't claim we *were* the friggin' United States Army!'

81

'It was only a Goddamn small town bank!' Shelby snarled.

Alice urged: 'Con, don't let these guys take over again. It's us oughta be givin' the orders.'

'Sure, Alice,' her husband replied absently, showed Edge a covert look unseen by anyone else. It was obviously intended to convey a tacit message, but Edge could not even start to guess what this was until he and Christie had searched through every saddlebag, come up with just the Colt taken from the half-breed's holster in the Western States Bank at Munro.

Edge switched the handgun with the one already in his holster. Then unloaded Banning's revolver, threw this on the wagon. Christie saw this, remembered the three guns he had claimed, took them out of various pockets and emptied each chamber of every cylinder. Consigned the weapons to the heap of gear behind the wagon seat.

'You old farts saw all that?' Alice asked as Edge and her husband moved away from the wagon and Christie gestured for the old-timers to get aboard the rig. 'You're gettin' back everythin' belongs to you. Except for the bullets. So you can't shoot at us. But you can come back later and get them if you want.'

'Much later,' Christie stressed. 'Long after we've left. Best you remember what I told you about Alice's skill with the rifle over long range. If you try to sneak back here too soon, it will be a bad mistake and——'

'Okay, okay, schoolteacher!' Shelby cut in impatiently. 'Rube didn't get through lecturin' your old lady. So you return the favour, uh? Save your lousy lectures for some unlucky bunch of kids out in California?'

He went to the wagon first, dragging his stiff leg, and hauled himself up on the back. Claimed a spot where he could squat down close to the body of Pete Race. He took off his own kerchief, draped it carefully over the face of the corpse as Duffy climbed on to the seat and Miller gave Banning a boost aboard.

'All being well, we won't have further need of loaded guns, young man,' Banning said when he was comfortably positioned between two saddles, rested a hand on a pair of bags attached to one of them. 'Even short the hundred and fifty Edge took back, I'm sure we have more than sufficient for our purpose.' He showed a beaming smile. 'I can't tell you it's been a pleasure doin' business with you people, but——'

'The hell with all that fancy talk, Rube!' Shelby complained. 'Get this rig rollin', Duff. Let's get on home, fix up a decent funeral for Pete.'

Duffy glanced down over his shoulder, waited for a nod of approval from Banning before he released the brake lever, cracked the reins to stir the team into motion. Steered them to the right of the derelict building, the Conestoga and the rock: on the fork of the trail that continued due west.

'You any good with a rifle, mister?' Alice asked. She sounded huskily breathless, her voice almost inaudible against the clop of slow-moving horses, clatter of turning wheels.

'Better than some, but I'm no marskman, lady,' he told her as he went to the lamp. Where he crouched, lowered the wick until the flame spluttered out.

'Shit, I'm only a hotshot at tincans and bottles or cardboard targets: stuff like that, mister. I ain't sure I could even bring myself to squeeze a trigger if a flesh and blood human bein' was in front of the gun!'

A shrill shout sounded from the wagon and it suddenly jolted to a halt.

Alice Christie rasped: 'Here!'

Edge turned and straightened up, managed to get his hands high enough to catch the rifle she flung at him.

Then she whirled and lunged toward her husband. He instinctively held his arms wide, took her into an embrace. Looked more frightened than her until he saw the half-breed aimed the rifle along the trail toward the halted wagon.

A moment later, Banning roared: 'You lyin' sonofabitch, Edge! You took it all!' He had to catch his breath because of the stifling effect of the high degree of his anger. 'You said we had a deal, you welchin' bastard!'

Edge threw the rifle to his shoulder, angled up and to the left. Triggered a shot and pumped the action. The series of metallic clicks sounded against the echo of the report and the ricochet off the granite face of Eagle Rock.

The horses in the traces of the wagon and the five hitched at the rear shied and snorted, tried to rear against their restraints. One of the men, the ill-tempered Shelby or maybe Duffy who had to struggle to get the spooked animals back under control, snarled a stream of profanity.

The half-breed shouted: 'Move on out! Or get taken back to Munro: dead or alive!'

The horses calmed and there was a brief silence, the tension aboard the wagon surely no higher than that which gripped the embracing couple to the right and slightly behind Edge.

'Rube?'

The name was whispered, but the strained voice sounded loud enough to carry through fifty yards of utter stillness.

'We're old, but we still got time enough to get our own back, Duff,' Banning's voice was heard as a kind of stage whisper, purposely pitched to reach Edge and the Christies.

'So, Rube?'

'He's sayin' to move the friggin' rig outta here, you dumb bastard!' Shelby snarled.

'Before time runs out for us, the same way it has for Pete,' Banning added.

'I'm all for that,' Miller encouraged bitterly.

'Do it, Duff.'

Banning gave the explicit instruction to the driver and the wagon started forward again at a sedate pace. The sound of it masked what was said next. Whatever, it resulted in a sudden spurt of speed that raised a cloud of dust which in the still, cold, moonlit air did not drift back to where Edge turned slowly, sloped the Winchester to his shoulder, said to the Christies:

'Obliged for everything so far.'

'I suppose we're not finished helping you yet?' the man asked, dropped his arm from around his wife's waist.

'I'm going to need all the money you took out of Banning's saddlebags, feller.'

'But are you gonna give it back to the bank?' Alice asked dully.

Edge rasped the back of a hand over the bristles on his jaw, answered in the same tone she used: 'You two ain't the only honest people in a dishonest world, lady.'

'I said I wasn't no lady.'

'It's equally true we're honest, Mr Edge,' Christie said. Gestured toward the Conestoga. 'The bags of stolen money are in our wagon.'

'We shouldn't just hand the loot over to him, Con.'

Edge patted the tied-down holster with the Colt in it, raised the Winchester barrel slightly from his shoulder, sloped it back again. 'Situation on who gives the orders has changed, Mrs Christie.'

The schoolteacher said: 'We have to take his word that he'll return the money to where it rightfully belongs, Alice.' He shrugged. 'And anyway it still will be none of our business once we go our separate ways.'

'Guess you're right,' she allowed and there was defeat in her tone, expression and even the way her shoulders fell. Like she felt she had irrevocably lost something: which made Edge wonder briefly what would have happened to the money if the old-timers had not returned to Eagle Rock as soon as they did.

'Unless!' Christie said suddenly, snapped his fingers, spread a smile insecurely across his lean features.

'Honey?'

He looked at Edge: 'You say this town where the robbery took place is just a few miles north east of here?'

'Three or four hours by wagon without rushing, feller.'

'So it won't delay us too much if we go back there with you?' His enthusiasm was abruptly tempered with nervousness when he added: 'No offence, but we'd know for sure then the money was returned to its rightful place?'

They were both tense as they waited for the half-breed's response. Immediately became calm when he lodged the Winchester in the crook of an arm, dug out the makings, then answered:

'How long before the happy event, Mrs Christie?'

The man was for some reason embarrassed, the woman perplexed by the inquiry as she looked down at herself, ran both splayed hands over her bulged belly.

'Oh, not for another three months at the earliest,' she answered.

Edge nodded. 'So I'll be glad to have your company on the trip back to Munro.'

'But what has my condition got to do with it?'

Edge pursed his lips, drawled: 'Already wanted for murder and bank robbery back there, Mrs Christie. Don't want to wind up holding any other kind of baby.'

The schoolteacher's embarrassment expanded at continued talk of the unborn child. But he was plainly easier in his mind when he curved an arm around the woman's waist again, admitted in a rush: 'Alice isn't Mrs Christie.'

Edge finished rolling the cigarette.

'I'm the father of the child, but I am married to another woman. The infant will be a ... it will be illegitimate.'

Edge struck a match on the jutting butt of his Colt, said evenly: 'So what the hell, feller?' He lit the cigarette, completed: 'For most of us all of life is pretty much of a bastard.'

10

Edge lent a hand with the few chores that had to be done to break camp at Eagle Rock: helped Conrad Christie put the four-horse team in the Conestoga traces while Alice, nervously clutching her own rifle, kept watch on the trail to the west where the old-timer's wagon had now gone out of sight into the distance and the darkness.

Without being asked, Christie showed Edge where the bulging gunnysack and the coin-clinking bags he had seen taken from the Munro bank had been stowed. They were in a drawer of an elegant rosewood writing bureau that looked to be the only quality item of furniture packed into the rear of the heavily laden covered wagon.

The half-breed told the eager-to-co-operate schoolteacher it would be all right for the stolen money to stay where it was.

It was not until they were rolling, the half-breed, the schoolteacher and the woman all crowded on to the high seat with Edge driving and searching for the sign that showed where Duffy steered the flatbed on to the trail, that Christie gave in to a nagging need to explain events at Eagle Rock.

'We were completely staggered, and not a little afraid, at what we found back there, Mr Edge. Those horses hobbled out behind the remains of the building. And the saddles piled up against the rock. It was totally unexpected, of course.'

'You don't have to sound so guilty about it, Con,' Alice protested from where she sat on the far end of the seat from Edge. She linked her arm possessively through Christie's.

'I know, Alice. But——'

'But nothin', honey. We didn't do anythin' wrong.'

'I know.' He sighed, not fully in agreement with her.

Edge drawled: 'You thought about it, I guess?'

'I never...' He started to sound affronted, then vented a

low sound of self-disgust, pointed out defensively: 'You can see our circumstances, Mr Edge. I have more or less admitted Alice and I are running away from commitments in Philadelphia, and we aren't exactly flush.'

'And we're only human,' Alice added softly.

Edge finished smoking the cigarette he had lit and let go out back at Eagle Rock, relit before they left. He tossed the butt off the side of the wagon, said on a trickle of exhaled tobacco smoke: 'It doesn't matter a damn to me, but you took a look in the saddlebags, found the money and were tempted to steal it. I can see how that could——'

'No!' Alice broke in vehemently. She leaned suddenly forward to look across Christie at Edge, her freckled, acne-scarred face set in a glower. 'It didn't happen at all like that. Did it, Con? Tell him, honey!'

'It wouldn't have happened at all in normal circumstances,' Christie said grimly as he stared straight ahead, seemed oblivious to the change of direction as Edge steered the rig off the trail. Perhaps saw juxtaposed against the night-shrouded middle distance vivid images of Philadelphia and Eagle Rock. 'Our team needed to be rested. We'd been pushing them harder than we should have through the mountains. We were so eager to get over the Rockies, for the mountains seemed to be the final serious obstacle between us and California.'

He shrugged. 'If we hadn't driven the horses so vigorously, I'm certain we'd have pressed on. Found another suitable place to stop for the night. When we saw the horses, I mean. But because...'

'Shit, I'm the woman!' Alice broke in. 'We're just naturally more out and out nosy and meddlesome than you men. It was me had to take a peek at what was in the saddlebags, Edge.'

She leaned forward to peer at him again, show him the earnest expression on her homely face. 'But I was lookin' for food, that's all. We haven't eaten anythin' but trail rations for weeks and ... Anyway, while Con was seein' after the team, I poked my nose in where it had no business bein'. And I found the money. I may be dumb, but I ain't out and out stupid. I knew from the way it was bein' carried, how the horses were left like they were for some reason, the money wasn't part of somethin' innocent and above board.'

'Sure, so like I said, you figured to steal it,' Edge reminded.

'No! No we did not!' Christie was angrily affronted now.

Alice looked again at Edge as she took a firmer grip on Christie's arm, said flatly: 'Con bein' a teacher and all, he'll know some fancy word to dress it up, maybe. All I can say: way I figure it, was a simple matter of finders keepers.'

Christie's outrage had calmed and his tone was even when he admitted: 'We're just attempting to justify acting in a way we knew was dishonest, I suppose. But we did impose a time limit on events, Mr Edge.'

'Right, we could have just gone on our way as fast as the winded team would take us,' Alice interjected eagerly.

'But we agreed we would wait until morning. And if no one came by then we'd presume as Alice said, that as finders of the money, we could keep it.'

'Damn right!' the woman rasped emphatically.

Christie hurried to qualify: 'Unless somewhere, some time later, we discovered who the money truly belonged to.'

'No sweat.'

'I'm sorry?'

'It's all in the past. You know who the money belongs to now, so it's all going to end for the best. And you'll both be able to live with your consciences after it's safely back in the Munro bank.'

'Yes, that is essentially correct, of course,' Christie agreed, nodded vigorously, no hint of regret in his tone.

'Sure is.' Alice sounded less convinced of what she said. But added with a tone of resignation: 'And like somebody said back there where we met up, I sure learned my lesson. From the mistake of figurin' little Alice Brown from Flatbush, Brooklyn could get her hands on a bundle of easy money.'

She shuddered. 'I sure couldn't've lived with myself if I'd had to shoot somebody. Maybe even killed him, my God!'

Christie nodded solemnly, said: 'It was too late for us to try to get away by the time I saw you and those other men coming along the trail on the wagon.'

'Through his telescope,' Alice put in. 'Con used to be a seafarer before he took up teachin' school.' It was like she was anxious to change the subject.

But Christie was eager to get the full story told now that he and the woman had explained the reason for their uncharacteristic behaviour at Eagle Rock. 'I counted the five of you, which matched the number of horses left at the abandoned building. I realised then all we could do was brazen it out and hoped I could explain everything as it had actually happened. But without any reference to Alice. I made her hide in the wagon. But I knew, of course, that if things got ugly, she would take a hand with the rifle.'

'I was prayin' to God in heaven I wouldn't have to. She sounded afraid, even at the memory of it.

Edge suppressed a query about when the money was taken from Ruben Banning's saddlebags: before he and the old-timers showed up at Eagle Rock, or while Christie was out back of the ruined way station on several occasions afterwards? For the answer was of no importance to Edge. Only to the states of mind of the couple riding on the seat beside him.

Alice Christie asked after a short pause: 'You don't have nothin' to offer in exchange for all the talkin' we been doin', mister?'

'Figured I said all I needed to say back there at Eagle Rock?'

'Yes, you did.' It was clear Christie would welcome a longer pause in their talk.

The woman pressed on: 'But a man of your... your style, Mr Edge? You had a gun, yet it was like you were some kind of prisoner. You let yourself be ordered around by that bunch of crippled old-timers.'

'Yes, that certainly seemed to be the case.' Christie was suddenly as interested as her in his answer. 'I think that as much as anything else added to the unreality of the situation.'

Edge replied with a note of finality in his voice: 'Yeah, I surprise myself sometimes.'

Edge thought Alice was intent upon pursuing the subject, but Christie made some kind of sign that she should abandon it. And this heralded a silence that hung much easier in the chill night air than any of those that had been clamped over the other wagon heading in the opposite direction.

It endured for several minutes while the three people on the seat remained content with his or her own thoughts. Then Conrad Christie ended it, asked as he began to peer to left and right instead of directly ahead:

'You're familiar with this part of the country, Mr Edge?'

'No.'

'Then how can you be sure you're going the right way back to...'

'Munro,' Alice supplied. Then laughed and taunted good naturedly: 'Schoolteachers might be real smart in some things, Con. But they don't know everythin'.' She raised an arm, swept it from side to side to indicate the terrain ahead. 'See how the moon, low the way it is tonight, makes clear shadows of everythin'? Includin' the wheel tracks left by the wagon Edge and them old-timers rode on?'

'Goodness, yes! What a fool, of course that's how he's doing it.' He looked sheepish.

It was clear why Christie had been so intrigued by the route Edge took since cutting off the trail. For by staying on the easiest, smoothest course chosen by Ed Duffy, the Conestoga often veered to left or right without apparent reason. And the skyline ahead constantly changed, so few distinctive landmarks were ever in view for long at a time.

'And other people sometimes surprise me,' Edge said after awhile.

Christie shook his head. 'I'm sorry?'

Alice, possessed of a native common sense that occasionally balanced the man's academic knowledge, told him: 'Like he said awhile back, Con, sometimes Edge surprises himself. And sometimes other people surprise him is what he's saying now. I'm one of that kind.'

When she looked quizzically across Christie at him, Edge said: 'I'd figured you were from New York.'

'Long before Philadelphia. So how come I know how to shoot a rifle well as I do? And how to read sign on the kind of terrain that's nothin' like anythin' close to New York or Philly?'

'It's no burning issue, but I guess it intrigues me a little.'

She leaned against the back of the seat, wriggled into a more comfortable position like she was getting set for a lengthy explanation. 'Born in Flatbush, mister. But after my Ma died when I was five Pa packed me off to live with his brother and his wife. Uncle Abe was town marshal of West Farmington, Kansas. I lived there with him and Aunt Josephine until I was near fifteen.

'Aunt Jo was always a pain in the . . . neck. Straitlaced as they come. But Uncle Abe, he was fine. At first. Taught me a lot. Includin' how to target shoot a rifle, track sign, hunt game, stay alive in the wild: stuff like that. But when I got to be fourteen and started to fill out the way some girls that age do, Abe tried to teach me some other kindsa stuff.'

'I'm sure Edge has the general picture, Alice.' The long faced, hollow eyed, sandy haired man in the shabby suit was even more embarrassed now. 'There's no need of the finer details.'

'What . . . ? Well, oh yeah. I guess I've said enough about that. So . . . After I ran away to Philadelphia—don't ask me why there, I just liked the sound of the name, far as I can recall—I didn't let what Uncle Abe tried to do to me turn me bad. Stayed honest and decent right up until I started to work for Con and his wife.'

She uttered a shocked exclamation when she realised how this could be misunderstood.

Christie admitted morosely: 'I suppose you can take that just the way it sounds, Mr Edge. She does mean I was the first man . . . of any consequence in her life. She was an innocent young parlour maid in our home until I took advantage of her.'

'You did not take advantage of me, Con!' she insisted and it was obvious the matter had often been raised between them.

'You know what?' Edge asked with a sigh, and the weariness he first experienced at Eagle Rock now gripped him again.

'What?' Alice asked and she sounded disinterested, impatient to go on with her account.

'Yes?' Christie was a little anxious.

'I've been around, met up with all kinds of people. Not one

of them was perfect and I'm no angel myself. I guess it'll be much the same after we've gone our separate ways.'

'I'm afraid I fail to grasp the point you are getting——'

'Usually, he'd just say no sweat, Con,' Alice broke in sourly. 'But this time he's sayin' in a roundabout way he don't give a damn about us. It don't matter to him if I was the most screwed whore in New York, Philadelphia and West Farmington, Kansas. Or if you corrupted every little girl you ever taught in class, Con.' She leaned forward to look at Edge. 'Ain't that about right, mister?'

'Just so long as you both tell the truth to the sheriff at Munro when I bring the money back to the bank.'

After a few moments of frowning thought the woman started sullenly: 'All I wanted to say was that——'

'Leave it alone, Alice,' Christie interrupted. Swung his head one way then the other to look at her, then the half-breed. 'You do well not to mince words, Mr Edge. That's perfectly all right with me. You made your point and I feel Alice and I have said sufficient to explain our positions. We are like ships that should have passed in the night. But since circumstances ordained otherwise there is absolutely no reason why we should admire each other. Or be in the least interested in our respective pasts.'

'I'll go along with that, feller.'

'I'm real sorry if all this talk has bothered you,' Alice muttered without contrition.

'No sweat,' Edge told her.

'Neither a man to mince words,' Christie said, trying for a lightness of tone. 'Nor, under normal circumstances, a man of more than a few of them.'

'I spend a lot of time alone, feller.'

Alice countered quickly: 'It sure is easy to see why.'

Christie made a shushing sound.

Edge nodded, murmured: 'From choice, usually.'

'So fine! We don't want to be nuisances to you, mister. If it's only a couple of hours until we get into town, I reckon even I can hold my tongue that long!'

Christie was still trying to introduce good humour into the atmosphere following the long period of tension and danger, his personal discomfiture at the public washing of dirty linen. And he said with the experience of a long-married man—albeit not married to the woman who carried his baby in her womb: 'Two hours, Alice? That surely will be something to behold.'

The half-breed murmured through pursued lips: 'It'll be some kind of a pregnant pause.'

11

Dawn had started to spread a dirty grey half-light across the solidly clouded night sky in the east when Conrad Christie asked:

'That smoke will be from Munro, I suppose?'

The woman was sleeping, her head tilted to rest on his shoulder. She had been like that for the past two hours. And Christie himself had been awake only for a few minutes; now the relatively smooth surface of the trail into Munro from the west was rolling under the slow-turning wheels of the wagon, since Edge turned the Conestoga up off the rough country to the south.

During the silent part of the ride, Edge had smoked three cigarettes and kept his mind devoid of every kind of thought. For there were too many variables in his immediate future: dependent upon making it uneventfully into Munro, then having the true account of what had happened believed by the local lawman and the people he was sworn to protect.

'Right, feller,' he confirmed after he glanced at the flat-topped pall of black woodsmoke that hung against the greyness of the dawn sky now that the blackness of night had almost totally faded.

'Country town people rise early.'

'Most of them eat early, too. And I sure could do justice to a plate of whatever's cooking on the stove of the hotel run by Mary Wilde.'

'The lady's obviously a good cook,' Christie said with much the same brand of hungry enthusiasm mixed with fatigue as sounded in Edge's voice.

'If her breakfast ham and eggs are as good as her supper chilli. I was pretty damn hungry then, also.'

'I certainly am now, Mr Edge. And not simply because it's

95

been so long since I last ate fresh food. More than that, I think, it's because I no longer have a bad taste in my mouth from what Alice and I almost did last night. I have you to thank for that. And I haven't properly expressed my appreciation until now.'

'Glad to know you feel that way, Christie. Means I won't owe you anything for the favour you're going to do me in town.'

There was a brief pause while the schoolteacher mulled over the half-breed's laconic response. Then, as the buildings that flanked the western end of Lark Street came into distant view beneath the thickening smoke pall against the lightening sky, he admitted:

'I've been thinking over much of what you've said, Mr Edge. And I consider you truly are a man of honour. Yet you . . .'

He turned to peer at Edge's heavily bristled profile. Seemed a little nervous, like he half expected a violent flare-up of anger from him. But Edge remained impassively silent and Christie finished what he had started to say.

'You give the impression of being . . . I mean your manner does not immediately engender a sense of trust in other people I suppose is what I mean.'

Again Edge did not respond to what was said of him, nor meet the quizzical look Christie directed at him.

Alice, who had given no sign until now that she was awake, muttered, her voice thick from sleep: 'Another lesson Uncle Abe taught me, Con. Out here, when a man makes it plain his business is his business, take the hint. Don't pry, honey.'

She straightened up on the seat, yawned, flexed her stiffened muscles, rubbed the crick from out of her neck.

Christie complained: 'Goodness, I do hope things are somewhat different in California. It sometimes seems one just cannot hold a civilised conversation on this side of the Mississippi!'

Edge spat sour-tasting saliva off the side of the wagon. Hoped his mouth, like that of Christie, might water in anticipation of a well cooked breakfast. Then he drawled: 'You figure maybe that's why they call it the Wild West?'

Christie gave a short, spontaneous laugh that sounded as much of released tension as appreciation of a joke. This as the wagon rolled close enough to Munro so they could hear the voice of a woman singing off-key in the back yard of a clapboard house where she was hanging out the wash.

'Hey, that's really funny!' He chortled again. 'Your kind of sardonic humour can be first class in the appropriate circumstances, you know.'

'Con, don't overdo the praise, honey,' Alice warned.

There was genuine concern in her voice and Edge thought he knew why she was so protective toward him. She may have been a woman who was considerably younger than the father of her unborn child. But she had led her short life in a way that gained her the kind of experience that was useful for much of what had faced them on the gruelling journey from Philadelphia, culminating in the dangerous confrontation at Eagle Rock. Whereas his breeding and book learning had probably counted for little in most such situations.

Now she was worried about how the strain he had been under for so long was obviously still contained within him: relieved just a little by his lightheartedness now he was within sight of a town he hoped was peopled by men and women with whom he shared an affinity. And if Munro disappointed his expectations, good humour would be a very fragile base for his new found confidence.

'Certainly, Alice,' he allowed, extricated his arm from hers so he could drape it around her shoulders, hold her more tightly to establish even closer contact. Like he was trying to protect her instead of the other way around. He grinned foolishly at her, then at the half-breed. 'But you have to admit, Mr Edge certainly can grow on you, don't you find?'

'So can warts,' Alice countered grimly. But she leaned forward to look across at Edge, expressed her equivalent of the half-breed's own cold grin to convey that she was half joking: if that was what he wanted.

Edge continued his narrow-eyed study of the town.

The white-aproned woman who was hanging out the laundry in back of the house on the north side of the end of Lark Street now heard the sound of the approaching wagon.

She peered out along the trail toward it, interrupted her chore to raise an arm, waved it fervidly in greeting.

'Look, Alice!' Christie exclaimed. 'The natives are friendly. Wave back!'

He used his free arm to do so. Alice did the same. And it was as if by doing so the two eager to be friendly Easterners disassociated themselves from the taciturn Westerner who continued to occupy both hands with the reins, driving the four-horse team at an easy pace toward Munro.

'No hard feelin's, uh?' Alice asked when the long-range exchange of greetings was over, the Munro woman went back to hanging the wash and the two people beside Edge took to looking at the town in general. 'A guy that hands it out, he oughta be able to take it too?'

'What's that?'

'The wisecrack I made about warts.'

'No sweat. And all is how you take me.'

Christie said: 'Munro looks to be a nice town.'

He was almost fully in control of himself now, but it was just discernible that he was still anxious over something. Probably, Edge thought, for their business with him to be completed. So maybe he was barely able to contain his excitement that it soon would be?

'It looks that way,' Edge allowed without interrupting his glinting-eyed study of the town, paying closer attention to detail than Christie and Alice. 'But maybe you should keep in mind what you said about the way I look.'

'What's that supposed to mean, mister?' Alice's voice was harsh-toned.

Christie demonstrated just how much of his composure he had regained, for he immediately recalled the reference, was able to tell her: 'I remarked how Mr Edge's appearance was deceptive.'

He did a double-take at Munro, found nothing at second glance to disturb him.

Roosters crowed, dogs barked, some horses whinnied as the early morning new arrivals in town drew nearer. And then the fleshily built woman with grey hair in a bun and a crimson complexion abruptly changed her attitude toward the newcomers as the wagon rolled off the open trail on to the western end of Lark Street, ran past the schoolhouse that was the first building on the south side of the street.

She still had a clear view of the rig as she straightened from stooping to pick up the empty basket. Seemed about to call a cheerful greeting but then did a pronounced double-take at the trio of people on the seat. And the bright smile on her unhealthily red face suddenly switched to a harsh scowl. Then she half turned, moved at an ungainly waddling run toward and through an open doorway at the rear of the house.

'What was that all about?' Christie asked, disappointment giving his voice a strangely shrill tone.

'It's not on our account, honey,' the woman beside him said, not quite able to mask her nervousness.

Edge confirmed: 'I'm the only bad penny that's just shown up around here.'

'Of course!' Christie was sheepish again at failing to realise the obvious.

Edge looked carefully along both sides of the street, deserted at this early hour of the morning. Since the animals had quietened and the woman banged the door closed, only the sight and smell of smoke from newly lit stoves signalled that much of the town was already awake.

Along the south side of the street beyond the schoolhouse at the rear of a walled play yard there was a church. Then four large two story houses, a line of half a dozen smaller ones, the law office and jailhouse, the Grand Hotel and three stores.

Next to the clapboard house with the wet washing hanging limp on the line out back was a blacksmith's forge, a bakery already giving off the fragrance of fresh bread, the town meeting hall, a building with several shingles flanking the double doorway, the Centennial Saloon, Western States Bank, some more stores, a stage line depot, telegraph office and Doyle's Corral and Livery Stables.

The buildings were mostly weathered granite or well preserved timber, some a mixture of the two. All were well maintained against the ravages of the Rocky Mountains climate. All looked to be locked up tight.

The clock Edge had heard faintly when he was locked in

99

the jailhouse last night now chimed five times as the wagon rolled down the centre of the street, across the front of one of the larger houses that had impressive porches but no front yards. After the final note sounded, the clop of hooves, clatter of turning wheels and the creaking of wagon timbers once more supplied the only body of noise to disturb the stillness along the entire length of the street.

Until a door creaked open, then slammed closed as Edge, Christie and Alice turned their heads sharply to look in the direction of the first sound.

Even when the door of Snyder's Grocery Store was once more as firmly closed as all the others along both sides of the street, the sense of eyes watching from countless secret vantage points was disconcertingly strong.

Aware of the renewed tension that had gripped the other two riders on the wagon, Edge knew there was not a hostile watcher at every curtained window, each silently cracked-open doorway, hidden around every corner. It was just the illusion created by the brittle surrounding silence that seemed to have a palpable presence in the chill morning air.

It was natural that the arrival in town of an old Conestoga at such an early hour would arouse curiosity. Destined inevitably to turn to unease and then more powerful emotions as gazes fell upon the familiar sheepskin-coated, Stetson-hatted figure of the unshaven, impassive-faced man who held the reins.

The lead horses of the team were level with the corner of the saloon and Edge was about to tug at the reins to steer the wagon toward the front of the bank when Harry Grimes showed himself. Stepped from the suddenly wrenched-open doorway of one of the small houses on the other side of the street.

He was unshaven, his hair was dishevelled, his black eyes were no longer shiny above the dark half circles that signalled lack of sleep. He had dressed hurriedly in pants, undershirt and boots. Wore no gunbelt, but his Remington was in his right hand, raised and trained on Edge as he ordered:

'Hold it right there! Reins down, hands up!' He started down the cement walk between two squares of lawn, toward

100

the gate in the front fence.

Alice gasped.

Christie started to make the pompous sounding protest: 'I should point out Edge would hardly have returned to your town if he——'

Behind unflinching impassiveness Edge experienced a brand of white-hot anger that seared to every nerve ending in his body, threatened to explode his racing mind to smithereens. But in that same instant he opened his hands to release the reins he concentrated the rage into an ice cold ball at the pit of his stomach. Which did not prevent him launching into a violent reaction against the man with the pointing gun; but it did keep him from powering into any act of mindless recklessness.

He started to unfold off the seat, to stand upright on the footboard of the wagon. Began to raise his hands. But curled the right one around the butt of the holstered Colt. Had the revolver out, levelled, hammer back, in a blur of speed.

Heard Alice Brown's cry of alarm and Christie's rasp of an uncharacteristic oath.

Saw the fear of death spread across Grimes' face as the lawman reached the gate in the picket fence.

Then both guns exploded shots and Edge felt his own features form involuntarily into a killer's grin. While his mind filled with genuine pleasure as for the first time since the trouble got started right here in this very town—just a few feet away behind the closed door of the Western States Bank—he violently grasped the opportunity to unleash his frustration.

He heard the bullet from the Remington of the small-town sheriff tear through the canvas cover of the Conestoga, clang against one of the metal household utensils inside. At the same instant as that from the Colt in his more experienced hand smashed into the cylinder of the other man's revolver.

Even at a range of better than twenty feet, it had enough velocity to wrench to the side the arm behind the gun hand. Then tear the weapon from the grip of Grimes who yelled in mixed pain and shock as the Remington sailed across the patch of crab-grassed lawn, dropped into a clump of dead flowers.

'Harry?' a woman shrieked frantically from inside the house.

'Dear God,' Christie gasped. 'Unreal!' It's all so totally unreal again!'

'Easy, Con,' Alice placated anxiously.

Edge slid the Colt, trailing smoke from the muzzle, back into his holster. Remained standing as he looked fixedly at the dishevelled, near exhausted, badly shocked lawman who stared back at him with bright-eyed horror, drawled evenly:

'You're an exceptional feller, Sheriff Grimes.'

The lawman was abruptly aware of how much his hand hurt from having the gun blasted out of it. And he shook it, sucked on the bruised fingertips, clamped the whole throbbing hand tightly under the opposite armpit. Only then was he able to transform his expression into a scowl of contempt before he snarled:

'You're under arrest for the murder of Nicky Cornwall!'

Edge ignored this, told him flatly: 'You aimed a gun at me twice and didn't kill me, Sheriff. I made an exception of you by not killing you. Because it suited my purpose. Now I'll be obliged if you'd hold still awhile: listen to what Mr and Mrs Christie here have to tell you.'

Whether in response to the falsehood about their marital status, or out of their increasing uneasiness in another tense situation, Conrad Christie and Alice Brown huddled more closely together on the seat.

Then a petitely-built, good-looking, black-haired woman of about Grimes' own age stepped from the doorway of the house behind him. When she saw the sheriff was still on his feet, not dripping blood on the cement walk, her expression of frantic anxiety altered to a hate-filled glare directed at Edge.

Grimes glanced over his shoulder, instructed tautly: 'Go back inside the house please, Laura.'

Christie attempted to take the heat out of the situation. 'If we may be civilised about this, I'm certain it can all be explained to the satis——'

'Shut your fancy mouth, dude!' the booming voice of Clara Cornwall roared from a newly-opened door two houses along

102

from where the lawman stood at one end of the walk, his wife at the other. 'Harry, do your damn duty and arrest that——'

'What the hell do you think my husband is trying to do, lady?' Laura broke in caustically.

The powerfully-built Cornwall woman demanded: 'Lock up that hard-nosed sonofabitch took a shot at you and killed my grandson, you hear me, Harry Grimes? Or I'll——'

'Hush up now, Clara,' Vaughan Jameson called from the doorway of the house next to hers. 'We've already had enough violence in Munro to last us awhile.'

Along both sides of the street, doors had opened in the wake of the gunshots. Heads were thrust forward, people stepped out across their thresholds. But none moved to converge on the area of the confrontation as Edge asked of Christie:

'You want to tell the sheriff about it, feller? Short and sweet, uh? While I get the money out of the back?'

Christie looked nervously up at Edge, seemed to have trouble squeezing out a sound past the fear that constricted his throat. The half-breed showed him a glinting-eyed stare, nodded, then swung down from the wagon to the blind side to Grimes.

The lawman snapped his head around, swept an intense gaze over his small front yard. He was searching for the Remington and failed to see it hidden deep in the clump of dead flowers.

Christie cleared his throat noisily, started a little shrilly: 'Sheriff, surely you should have realised——'

'Short and sweet, Con,' Alice reminded gently. Turned her head to look earnestly down at Grimes' wife who was advancing fast along the wall, concerned to find out exactly how her husband had been hurt. Maybe to stop him looking more carefully for his revolver: finding it and putting himself in danger again.

'Edge didn't rob the bank here in town and he never had nothin' to do with killin' your young deputy, Sheriff,' Alice said. Her voice was pitched loud, and the tone held a warning she would not allow herself to be interrupted until she was through. 'He just happened to be in the bank when that bunch

103

of old fa...timers held it up. And then when the rest of them came back here to get their buddy outta the jail, there was no one around to see Edge didn't have nothin' to do with the killin'. So he figured his best bet was to take off with all of them.'

Edge groaned softly as he heard the second part of her hearsay account. He knew it could have been better phrased to avoid ambiguity. But as he climbed up into the rear of the covered wagon, conscious of so many belligerent gazes focused on him, he realised that now was not the time for subtle meanings and crystal clear understanding. No matter what Alice Brown said or how she said it, the townspeople's suspicion of him would remain solid until they were presented with physical proof of what she claimed.

He slid open the drawer of the elegant rosewood desk, took out the gunnysack of bills and two bags of coins. Noticed inconsequentially in passing that Grimes' bullet had dented a tin hip bath.

Outside, Alice made to expand on what she had said. But she was hushed into silence by Christie who raspingly pointed out she had already done what Edge asked: stated his case in a nut shell.

As he climbed down from the rear of the wagon and approached the gateway where Harry and Laura Grimes stood, he was once more the centre of mistrustful attention. And he wondered if anyone noticed both his hands were occupied with the bags of money. So it was not possible for him to make a fast draw now.

The wife of the sheriff expressed fear. Grimes started to show a glimmer of uncertainty behind his hard-eyed expression and when Edge thrust out both hands, he instinctively made to take the proffered bags. But he could manage only the gunnysack of bills with his left hand. His bruised right one would not close.

'Ma'am,' Edge said, held out the coin bags toward the startled Laura.

'Take them, honey,' Grimes instructed huskily.

Edge said: 'You'll need to have the woman from the bank check if it's all there. If it ain't, I didn't take what's missing.'

104

'Nor neither did we, if that's what you're inferrin', mister!' Alice snapped irately.

'Implying,' Christie corrected automatically, like it was something he did often.

Grimes growled: 'I'm going to need more than this. And hear more than has been said so far. Before I'll drop the charges against you, mister.'

'I can go along with that, Sheriff,' Edge allowed. 'I'll be at the hotel along the street for awhile. Need to wash up, eat, get me some sleep. I can talk while I do the first two. Talk better after all three.'

The big-built, gleaming-eyed Clara Cornwall had emerged from her house, strode down the walk of her front yard. Now she slammed her gate behind her ample figure, swung to advance on Edge and the Grimes. Yelled:

'What kinda town d'you think this is, mister? You really figure our elected peace officer is gonna wait on the pleasures of a bank robber and killer before he does his duty?'

'Mrs Cornwall I...' Laura started.

'Clara,' the sheriff broke in on his worried wife. 'I reckon we should all just calm down some and take it——'

'What we should all do is string up this no good saddletramp, that's what we should do!' the bombastic woman roared. She snapped her head one way, then the other: blazing eyes commanding support for the contention from her fellow citizens.

A rising swell of talk had gotten started after the bags of money changed hands. This was suddenly curtailed and utter silence was clamped down along the length of Lark Street.

Edge, still aware of simmering inner tension even after he eased his feelings to some extent by blasting the gun out of Grimes hand, gave in to an overwhelming impulse to recklessness.

He drew his Colt.

Heard the mass gasp released by many throats. Then came another silence as he gripped the barrel of the gun with his left hand, let go of the butt from his right. Turned the gun fast, spun slowly on his heels, and thrust it toward the incensed woman.

The crimson glow of anger suddenly drained out of her face, left her skin chalk white, her mouth gaping wide, unable to vent the abuse she had it in mind to hurl at him.

'Edge!' Christie had cried when he saw the draw.

'Oh, shit,' Alice rasped at the same time.

They both gulped noisily when they witnessed the switch of the gun from hand to hand.

The Grimes were as dumbstruck as Clara Cornwall.

'You really think I killed your grandson the boy deputy, lady,' Edge asked icily, 'take the gun and kill me back.'

It was a crazy play, he knew. Even as he spoke he was awesomely aware he could have totally misjudged this woman. She might just be grief-stricken enough over the violent death of her grandson to be equally reckless. Think only of vengeance as she snatched the gun from him, blasted a bullet into him.

And for a stretched second she was no more than a heartbeat away from doing that. He was certain he read this in the depth of her pale grey eyes while the pulse raced in her throat. Then she managed to snap her sagging mouth closed, cleared her throat and forced out in a voice that sounded painfully strained:

'Hell, mister! Everythin' sure does seem like you're guilty as sin!'

Christie said timorously: 'You should not judge by appearances, Mrs Cornwall.'

Edge allowed pent-up breath to whistle out through pursed lips. Then transferred the Colt from one hand to the other again, slid it back in the holster.

He took the makings from his shirt pocket. Looked up and down the quiet street lined with people who returned his bleak-eyed gaze with deep shock rather than the suspicion that had showed on their faces before.

Then he rasped a hand over his unshaven, dirt ingrained face, grinned up at Christie, growled: 'That sure is right, feller. Reckon I ain't good looking, but right now I'm looking good.'

12

Edge thought the granite-built, plain-fronted, two-story Grand Hotel was probably appropriately named for a town like Munro: a small, isolated community, little more than one street, in the Rocky Mountains of Colorado's south western corner.

Anyway, that early morning it catered grandly enough for what he needed to fulfil the requirements he listed to Harry Grimes. Modest enough requirements supplied by a lady with a somewhat studied grand manner.

Mary Wilde looked at first impression to be in her early thirties, but maybe she could have been as old as fifty. She was a handsome rather than beautiful woman. A pale-complexioned understated blonde who carried herself with a kind of too stiff grace. Talked that way, too. So possessed a demeanour that perhaps by design would maybe aggravate and even alienate certain kinds of guests likely to stop by this small-town hotel. But Edge accepted this as her way: not aimed to make him feel uncomfortable because he was dirty, unshaved and probably smelled pretty high, too.

What he actually liked about Mrs Wilde was that although she surely knew much of what had happened to him in the time since he walked into the Western States Bank yesterday and when he came down the street toward her hotel this morning, she did not allow this to affect anything she said or did. She seemed incurious about him, and was not prepared to prejudge him. So long, he guessed, as he treated her and her establishment with respect. And could pay the bill at the end of his stay at the Grand Hotel.

She kept clean and comfortable rooms in which a guest with the reasonable price of the service could take a bath in luxuriously hot water supplied by a deaf-mute black man of great age who smiled a lot.

As Edge smoked a cigarette while he soaked in the scummy water after he had washed the dirt of so many miles on the trail off his body and shaved, it would have been easy to give into the enticing attraction of sleep for awhile. But then the cooling water in the chill morning began to make the prospect less tempting by the passing moment. So soon he was down in the small, neat dining room to one side of the elegant lobby: eagerly eating two fried eggs, four slices of ham, and a heap of grits. Washed down with the best-tasting coffee he could remember.

Mary Wilde cooked a breakfast as good as the supper of the night before.

It was an inviting notion as he sat alone in the dining room with a satisfyingly full belly to hope that the owner of the hotel was representative of the entire population of Munro. In how she had been toward him once he entered the closed but unlocked double doors of the Grand Hotel, to be welcomed just like any ordinary passing-through stranger to town who stopped by her place.

That had immediately struck a chord of affinity in Edge. And as he sat smoking after the fine breakfast, he thought idly that Mary Wilde could give Conrad Christie a few pointers on how to respect the privacy of people west of the Mississippi: or anywhere else for that matter. You had to take them at face value and not ask questions: unless they did anything that called their values into question.

Since he had been given an upstairs room at the rear of the hotel—Mrs Wilde suggested this because it would be much quieter for daytime sleeping—he had not been able to hear if anyone came and went through the lobby while he was getting himself cleaned up. As he ate breakfast, though, he did hear the double doors of the hotel open and close a number of times, muted footfalls on the carpeted floor of the lobby, muffled exchanges.

Because of the timing—David Doyle tentatively entered the dining room, just as he crushed out the cigarette butt in the brass ashtray on the white linen tablecloth—Edge was inclined to think Mary Wilde had kept a restraining eye on

108

the liveryman, held him at bay until her guest had finished breakfast.

The sixty-year-old, heavily-built, spade-bearded man with dull, slitted eyes and a mean mouth brought a faint, not unpleasant smell of horses into the stove-heated room still redolent with well-cooked food and strong coffee. He had on his leather work apron, toyed nervously with his hat in both hands and looked a little browbeaten: like he had been given some kind of low-keyed ticking off by the staid owner of the hotel.

'Mrs Wilde said it was okay for me to stop by, see you in here, mister?' There was just a hint of the disgruntled in his tone.

Edge nodded it was all right with him, too. 'You take good care of my horse and gear, feller?'

'Takin' good care of horses is about the only thing I'm any good at, mister. And you won't have nothin' to complain about when you see him, I'm thinkin'. I kept the saddle and your other stuff safe at the livery. You didn't say nothin' about doin' anythin' to it. Nor the sheriff didn't, neither.'

'You want to be paid now for what you've done?'

Doyle blinked his slit eyes, obviously disconcerted to have the point of his call raised by the other man. 'Uh?'

'Plan to stay another day, maybe a night, here in town. I can pay now what I owe for last night and——'

As Edge rose from the chair, he had started to take a wad of bills from his hip pocket.

Doyle's eyes widened to their restricted extent when he saw the money, then he blurted across what the half-breed was saying: 'Hell, no! Mrs Wilde, she said you was okay for money. It's just I wasn't sure how I stood. After Harry Grimes said the county wouldn't pay my bill. After you busted outta the jail. You're an honest man, mister. It's a pleasure to do business with someone like you. And if you want to stay a whole lot longer, pay for livery service by the week'll be fine with me. Don't want it in advance. Thanks, Mr Edge. I really appreciate it.'

He turned and hurried out, started to whistle as he closed the door behind him. Not loud enough to mask the refined voice of Mary Wilde as she boasted:

'There, did I not tell you as much, Doyle?'

After the liveryman left the hotel, still whistling his pleasure, she entered the dining room. Asked if Edge had enjoyed the food, then talked about the weather as she gathered up the dirty dishes and cutlery on to a tray. Continued to treat Edge just as if he had not been involved in the untoward happenings in this quiet backwater town. On her way out, though, she paused and said over her shoulder as an unimportant afterthought:

'By the by, Mr Edge. The couple who came into town with you this morning? They are also staying here at the Grand.'

Edge had last seen Conrad Christie and Alice Brown still talking with Grimes as he came down the street and most of Munro's citizens resumed their interrupted morning routines.

'Obliged for the information, ma'am.'

'They have taken rooms and are presently bathing.'

'Fine.'

It was clear she was working around to making a point: one, perhaps, she found it distasteful to raise.

'The gentleman told me to tell you there has been a long conversation with our sheriff. Mr Grimes appears to be perfectly satisfied all is as it should be in the matter of your unfortunate involvement with yesterday's distressing events.'

'Even finer.'

'I thought you would like to know this at the earliest.'

'Obliged.' Then, as she made to leave, he added: 'Ma'am?'

'There is something else you require? More coffee, perhaps?'

'You said the Christies took *rooms*—more than one?'

For the first time, Mary Wilde displayed an attitude that was something less than professionally friendly toward a hotel guest. She almost bristled with indignation as she countered:

'*Christies*, balderdash, Mr Edge! I have been in this business for long enough to pride myself I can judge whether a couple are man and wife or not. And those two are certainly not married in the eyes of God. I therefore insisted they take separate rooms. Or seek somewhere else to board in Munro.

110

Of course, it is amply evident the woman is heavily with child. But since the infant was not conceived under my roof, that is no concern of mine.'

She carried the laden tray out now. But before she could close the dining room door the front doors of the hotel opened. And it was like she saw something about the newcomer that caused her to turn, frown at Edge when she warned:

'Kindly keep it in mind, sir. I run an orderly house here. If there is the slightest hint of impropriety of any kind, I reserve the right to evict the guest responsible.'

She began to reshape her expression into an amiable smile as she looked toward the newcomer, greeted brightly: 'Good morning to you, Miss Terry. It seems set to be a fine one for the time of year, I think?'

'Yes, it does, Mrs Wilde,' Donna Terry agreed, just a slight trace of forced friendliness in her tone. It sounded a little more pointedly strained as she went on: 'Did you hear how your Mr Jameson took a hand with the trouble this morning? Did what he could to calm down that Clara Corn——'

'He is not *my* Mr Jameson!' Mrs Wilde broke in icily. 'Why does everyone in this town always make comments like that?'

She moved away from the dining room doorway, muttering irritably under her breath, the crockery and cutlery on the tray rattling with the shaking of her hands.

A moment later the blonde, blue-eyed, attractively slender Donna Terry took her place. For a stretched second her expression remained neutral. Then, when she was sure her face could not be glimpsed by the older woman, she showed a caustic scowl, closed the door, pressed her back to it like she was afraid Mrs Wilde would try to burst it open.

'They've been seeing each other for twenty years and perhaps old Vaughan has never even held her hand,' she said in a rasping whisper. 'But she's got no right to more or less accuse me of coming here to...'

She suddenly remembered exactly why she had come here. Recalled the last time she had been in the same room with the man who sat, silently impassive at the table. Now needed to use her vexation as a cover for embarrassment as she said:

'But why should you be interested in the small-minded gossip of Munro, Mr Edge? I've come to apologise to you.'

She remained at the closed door, perhaps additionally disconcerted because he did not stand up in the presence of a woman, as she had come to expect of the men she knew.

'You get to count the money yet?' he asked her flatly.

'Yes! Yes, I did. It's all there, down to the last penny.' She sounded breathless.

Edge nodded, reminded her: 'The name of the lady is ——'

'Miss Nancy Raven and she works... Miss Raven lives at a house... a place called Heaven's Gate in Cheyenne, Wyoming. Yes, I remember what you told me, Mr Edge. And I'll see to it your business is transacted just as soon as the telegraph office opens later this morning. You can rely on me to do that.'

'I'm obliged.'

She drew in a deep breath, chewed on her lower lip, then said in a rush: 'And I'll be obliged if you'd say you accept my apology for what happened at the bank yesterday, Mr Edge. I'm really so terribly sorry for the way I so totally misunderstood your part in the robbery. And even how...'

She lifted a trembling hand, ran the fingertips down her cheek: traced on her own skin the line of the scar that showed on the element-burnished surface of Edge's recently shaven face. 'If I had only known you were trying to protect the money and me——'

Edge pushed back his chair, rose to his feet now, told her: 'Forget it, lady.' He smiled with his mouth as he added: 'Like all us heroes are supposed to say: it's only a scratch.'

The humour was lost on her as she turned to open the door, acknowledged after a gulp: 'Thank you so much. If there is anything at all I can do for——'

'Don't make such a song and dance over it,' he said as Mary Wilde swept by Donna Terry to enter the dining room. She carried a tray stacked with everything necessary to lay up a table for two for breakfast. 'It's real nice of you to offer, but I'm going to bed down now, catch up on a lot of lost sleep. And the way I feel, I won't need any rocking.'

Mrs Wilde's head snapped sharply from side to side as she

peered frostily at Edge and the younger woman. Saw he grinned while she blushed.

The half-breed added as he went between the two of them and through the doorway: 'And rolling ain't allowed.'

13

As far as he was aware, Edge slept a dreamless sleep from close to six o'clock in the morning until six in the evening. His unmoving form luxuriously sunk into the down-filled mattress on a big double bed in an upstairs back room of the Grand Hotel.

Because the Winchester was still with the rest of his gear at the livery stable he slept with his Colt under the blankets, his right hand draped loosely around the revolver butt. Felt not at all like an over-cautious fool when he woke after so many undangerous hours; fully refreshed, with total recall of where he was and why he was there.

He dressed quickly against the Rocky Mountain fall air: even the Grand Hotel did not run to stoves in the bedrooms rented out to guests. Heard everyday domestic sounds far off within the building and caught the faint aroma of roasting meat. But the delicious smell did not detract from his first priority: the need to slake a thirst for a shot or two of hard liquor that he experienced from the tip of his tongue to the pit of his belly.

Out of the room, moving along the landing then down the stairway into the lobby, the appetising fragrance of pot-roasting beef grew stronger. He traced the murmur of talk to beyond a doorway on the other side of the lobby from the dining room, recognised the voices of Conrad Christie and Mary Wilde.

After he stepped out through the double doorway into the moonless night, turned left to move along the porch that ran the full width of the building, he glanced through the net-curtained window of a lighted room. Glimpsed Christie and the Grand's owner, with Alice Brown, seated at a table in a finely furnished parlour-style room. There were stem glasses

114

filled with pale-coloured liquid and an almost empty crystal decanter on the table.

A trickle of easy laughter at something Alice said sounded as Edge moved by, and he was briefly pleased for Christie that the schoolteacher had found at least one Munro citizen with whom he could converse in the style he had missed since he ran away from his wife in Philadelphia to be with the girl he had gotten pregnant.

The lack of a moon, obscured by a blanket of thick cloud, was hardly noticeable in town. For many windows spilled bright lamplight; stores that were still open and houses where supper was being prepared.

It was quiet along the entire length of Lark Street and the two narrower, shorter side streets that cut off to the north. A comfortable quiet, a world removed from the tension-crackling silence which had gripped the town when he drove the Conestoga in this morning.

There was even a brand of almost festive cheerfulness about the lights that shone out across the sidewalks. This probably created, he thought, by the way he was greeted with smiles, raised hands and an occasional word when he happened to glance in through open store doorways, pass people on the street.

These people hurried to get in out of the cold night air, begin what needed to be done at this evening time of the day.

The half-breed strolled without haste, allowing the cold bite of the air to increase his need of whiskey. Likewise it heightened his appetite.

He noticed, without letting it sour his mood of well being, how just a lone candle flickered in a window of the house where Clara Cornwall lived.

When he angled across the street toward the Centennial Saloon he heard a body of sound that conveyed there was quite a crowd in the place: and few of them were mourning the death of Mrs Cornwall's grandson.

Then the talk and the laughter, clink of glasses and rattle of coins faltered but did not end as he showed himself at the batwinged entrance, pushed through without a pause, moved toward the bar counter as the doors flapped closed behind him.

There were a score or so patrons in the saloon, and for a few seconds several nervous glances were switched between him and the centre of the counter where Harry Grimes stood, looking a lot less weary than when Edge last saw him. The sheriff used his left hand to drink beer while his right hung at his side, white bandages wrapped around three fingers.

Doc Salmon, who had doubtless dressed the bruised hand, was on one side of Grimes, David Doyle the other.

'What can I get you?' The fat and forty, snub-nosed, small-eyed, thickly-moustached bartender had moved to stand opposite Edge near the front end of the counter that ran along the right wall of the square, smoke-layered, well-lit and reasonably clean saloon.

'Rye whiskey?'

The bartender nodded, reached under the counter, produced a bottle and a shot glass, filled the glass from the bottle. 'Be ten cents.'

'I'll take care of that, John,' Sheriff Grimes said.

John, who seemed to be a man slow to smile, shrugged his meaty shoulders, made to replace the bottle under the counter. Edge reached for it, said:

'Leave it, John. I'll pay for what I drink.'

'Good God, man, why dinna you accept Harry's peace offering and let bygones be bygones?'

Now there was a sudden drying up of other conversations as the Scotsman's heavily accented voice, raised in something akin to exasperation, drew anxious attention from all parts of the saloon.

The liveryman who was one of those at the centre of this attention, looked like he wanted to turn and run out of the place. He gulped down his beer instead.

Edge said to the group of three men at the centre of the counter: 'The sheriff and me don't have any quarrel, I figure. Whatever was between us evened out. I pay my own way is all.'

Salmon's thin, grey-moustached face beneath his neatly-trimmed black hair expressed a scowl of anger. He made to reach out and grip the injured hand of Grimes, like he intended to hold it up, illustrate the unnecessarily violent way

116

the half-breed had evened out the score.

But Grimes spoke before the glowering Scot could get out the words around the rising anger in his throat: 'Suit yourself, mister.'

'I usually do, Sheriff,' Edge replied. He tossed down the drink at a swallow, uncorked the bottle to pour another. When the glass was brimful and the noise level rose again in the saloon, he turned to look at Grimes, suggest: 'We can talk some about law business? Without anyone getting in any one else's debt?'

'Sure.' Grimes finished his beer, said as he set down the glass: 'Another draught, John. One for the doc and Dave Doyle if they want.' He looked around for a convenient table, nodded toward one in the rear corner at the end of the bar counter. 'Suit you?'

'Sure.'

Edge carried the bottle of rye and glass to the table, aware the doctor was whispering low-toned advice to the sheriff, who listened without paying too much attention as he waited to get his beer. When it came he placed a heap of coins on the counter top, said something to John, moved to follow the half-breed.

When he was seated directly across the table from Edge, it was Grimes who spoke first, eager to make a point.

'I was a damn fool this morning, I know it.'

'You were?' Edge did not need to work at an intonation that made the remark a query instead of a bald statement of agreement with Grimes' self-criticism.

'Way you rolled into town so large as life—and you can't get a much bigger rig than that prairie schooner the Christies ride on—I should've done a little talking before I pulled a gun.'

'Conrad Christie tried to tell you that. But it was too late by then, I guess.'

He nodded, held up the hand with the bandaged fingers: 'You'd already done this. It was a pretty damn drastic thing to do, but it's your way of doing things. I'm sure not going to carry a grudge.'

'Fine.' Edge said and took out the makings.

Grimes' pale-complexioned face under the unfaded auburn hair spread with a personable smile as he qualified: 'Though I can't promise the same for Laura. We've not been married six months yet and she still thinks part of a wife's duty is to mother a husband. You damaged me, so she's not feeling too kindly to you.'

Edge felt good enough himself to counter evenly: 'Tell her that even though I don't like to be thought badly of by a beautiful woman, I can understand why I'm not her favourite person right now.'

'And I can't be sure Clara Cornwall is convinced you're totally blameless over what happened to young Nick,' Grimes said earnestly. All trace of humour was gone as he spoke about the death of the youngster he had obviously held in high regard.

Edge continued to feel well enough disposed toward the sheriff and the town in general not to voice the first facile response that occurred to him: about not caring so much about how a fat old lady regarded him. Instead: 'Maybe I can help you find the fellers responsible for that kid getting himself shot?'

Grimes took a swig of beer, then covetously eyed the other man's bottle of whiskey. Edge pushed the bottle across the table, completed rolling a cigarette while he watched the lawman drain the beer, pour himself a not over-generous measure of liquor into the large glass. Then Grimes said as Edge struck a match on the wall nearby, lit the cigarette:

'Right. I've been wasting time and you want to talk law business. But I have to tell you, me and the posse did our best, mister. Was out most of yesterday afternoon, late into the night. Trying to find sign after the bank robbery. Then most of us headed out again after we got back, heard about the jailbreak and young Nicky getting killed. Lost those tracks, too.'

He shrugged, grimaced, growled: 'Munro's not usually the kind of town that needs a smart lawman with hot-shot tracking skills. Not usually it ain't.'

Edge did not respond to the excuse. Instead asked: 'Christie tell you about Eagle Rock? Out on the trail that runs

118

south of the one comes through town?'

'Sure he did. And I'll be heading on out that way with a posse at first light tomorrow. None of us were fit to ride worth a damn this morning after all that time spent trying to pick up tracks in the dark yesterday. The time we lose letting the trail west of Eagle Rock get cold'll be made up for by us all being fresh when we start the manhunt again, I figure.'

Edge had taken his two shots of whiskey. Now he re-corked the bottle, ignored the way the sheriff eyed it enviously again. He was not prepared to buy more than the one drink for Grimes because of the disconcerting pang of conscience at how he had over-reacted to the man's own over-reaction early this morning.

Grimes made to expand on his excuse: 'I don't see how anyone could've done much more than us to——'

'That's not the matter I was going to bring up...' Edge started, then allowed his voice to trail away as a distant shout penetrated the steady buzz of sounds in the saloon. A shout that he sensed, rather than heard, meant all was no longer as it should be outside on Lark Street.

'You were saying, Edge?' Grimes prompted, just a little surprised at how the half-breed's attention had wandered and his voice had drifted away on a trickling exhalation of tobacco smoke. Against the body of background noise in which he had heard nothing out of the ordinary.

Then he suddenly grimaced, rasped: 'Aw, shit!'

The massive explosion first shook the saloon from roof to foundations, everything and everyone between the two. Then, a split second later, made itself heard.

Curses and shrieks of alarm were vented in a strident uproar in the wake of the blast. Counterpointed from outside the Centennial by the yells and screams of other Munro citizens.

Inside the building as the roar of the explosion continued to reverberate, men powered upright, whirled from where they stood. Froze and focused shocked attention on the rapidly flapping batwings through which billowed a dark cloud of dust and smoke acrid with explosion fumes.

Then footfalls trampled the floor in a stampede toward the

doorway. Men cursed each other as they collided painfully, tripped over their own feet.

Now other sounds could be heard outside: first the snorts of abused horses, then the beat of galloping hooves, last a fusillade of gunshots.

The rush for the batwings abruptly halted when somebody screamed and staggered back from the doorway. Men stumbled to either side, frantic to avoid contact with the man who swung his hands up to his neck. But he was not able to staunch the gush of blood from the bullet wound in his throat. A torrent of crimson that signalled the jugular had been holed.

'It's Dave Doyle, Goddamnit!' somebody yelled as the liveryman's staggering backward run ended and he sprawled heavily on his back across a table that collapsed beneath his weight.

For a stretched second while gunfire, galloping hooves, shouts and screams continued to sound outside, silence was clamped over the saloon. Until Doc Salmon shouldered his way through the press of stunned men crowded around Doyle's spreadeagled form on the smashed table.

He announced dourly after a brief examination: 'I fear David is dead, God rest his soul.'

Only now, as he moved without haste toward the doorway after he waited until the renewed stampede was over, did Edge realise he was probably the only armed man in the Centennial. But just with the Frontier Colt that was virtually useless when he pushed out between the batwings. In time to watch a tightknit group of riders racing out of town to the east. In a scene, he guessed, that was not dissimilar to the two violent incidents yesterday. Except the direction of escape both those times had been to the west. And this was more like the bank robbery than the jailbreak, for no wagon was being used.

Tonight it was again the turn of the Western States Bank, across the alley from the saloon. From inside the open doorway and blast-shattered windows of the building, came the flickering light of a small fire and the acrid taint of black powder smoke: the aftermath of the explosion used to force open the safe.

For many seconds as he stood directly outside the empty saloon, Edge felt himself totally detached from the raucous noise and frantic activity along the length of this street that just minutes ago he had found so comfortingly quiet. He felt this to such an extent he had a compelling urge to swing around and re-enter the saloon. Go back to the table he had shared with Grimes, pour himself another rye whiskey and drink it slowly while he finished smoking the cigarette.

Thus would he plainly demonstrate to the people of Munro—and prove to himself—that he no longer wanted any part of the violent troubles of this town.

Then he glimpsed a slight movement on the porch of the Grand Hotel. Felt his eyes forcibly drawn to focus on this one point despite all else that was taking place between and beyond.

A white-clad figure had stepped put through the double doorway of the hotel as a rifle shot sounded, seemingly in isolation from the pandemonium all round. And the white fabric was suddenly stained bright crimson before the form abruptly disappeared from sight back over the threshold.

He recalled that the only person dressed in white he had seen at the Grand Hotel was Alice Brown when she sat at the table in the finely furnished parlour. Said something funny that triggered laughter from the cultured father of her unborn child and the straitlaced hotel owner.

And now, for a reason he could not right then understand, Edge felt a sudden involvement with what was happening in Munro tonight.

'Damnit, Harry, they hit the bank again!' somebody in the crowd out front of the saloon snarled unnecessarily as the riders raced their mounts into the darkness clear of town to the east. And the level of noise rapidly diminished.

Somebody else said bitterly: 'And they reckon lightning don't strike in the same place twice!'

Edge took the cigarette out of the corner of his mouth, dropped it and ground it out under the sole of his boot. He growled sourly: 'They also reckon it never rains but it pours. But it doesn't get much done, talking up a storm.'

14

Three people died in Munro that night: four if the embryo child forming inside Alice Brown's womb was included in the tally.

For in addition to the mother-to-be and the liveryman, Paul Smith who owned the local tailor's store had also been fatally shot down by the gunfire as the bank robbers raced out of town with the money that was first stolen yesterday.

Edge reflected on the death toll and much more as he sat in the Centennial Saloon, far less crowded, much less brightly lit and a lot quieter than earlier: after Harry Grimes and his usual six-man posse had set out to track the killers and bank robbers who were, at least a half dozen witnesses claimed, the same old-timers who hit the Western States yesterday afternoon, then the jailhouse later. There was little doubt, many more witnesses said, they all wore kerchief masks and one or two of them seemed long past their prime as they clung to their galloping horses, fired off guns wildly to either side and over their shoulders. The number in the gang, according to reports, varied from three to ten.

Edge overheard some of these excitedly blurted accounts as he moved incuriously along the street, the people's voices raised to catch the attention of the grim-faced sheriff. While Grimes was plainly less concerned right then with the identities and number of the culprits than in a body count of their victims and rounding up a posse to go after them.

The half-breed was one of a dozen or so people who gathered out front of the Grand Hotel. Able to look in through the open double doors to where Conrad Christie was down on his haunches, starting to lift the lifeless figure of Alice Brown off the carpeted floor.

'The woman is quite dead, you ghouls!' the incensed Mary

Wilde accused shrilly when she saw the people peering in over the threshold of her hotel. 'She and the tiny mite she was carrying!'

By luck or a well placed shot, the pregnant woman from Brooklyn via West Farmington Kansas and Philadelphia Pennsylvania had been hit in the heart. Blood had spurted then oozed in such a way it vividly coloured only the swell of her left breast: obscenely emphasised its conical shape against the stark whiteness of the tight fitting bodice of her dress.

'I only came here to see if you were hurt, Mary!' the squeaky-voiced Vaughan Jameson sought to explain his presence at the scene of the tragedy.

The short, rubicund complexioned store-keeper–Edge had seen his name above the dry goods emporium next to the blast-shattered bank–had the nine- or ten-year-old Ellen with him again. He rested a protective hand on her narrow, slightly trembling shoulder: but did not think to shield her from the tableau within the hotel lobby.

Mary Wilde's censuring glower remained firm set when she heard this, then she made to swing the two doors closed. But something in Christie's tone caused her to hold back, stare hard at the schoolteacher who stood upright now, cradling the corpse of the newly-dead girl tenderly in his arms. His moist eyes directed their gaze at Edge as he insisted in a dull monotone:

'It's all my fault. If I hadn't asked Alice last night to ... If she hadn't used the rifle the way she did against ... They wouldn't have killed her. It was out of spite, I'm sure of it.'

Deep disgust with himself and tightly controlled rage at Alice's killer seemed a combination powerful enough to sap the final reserves of his strength. Threatened to drag him to the floor under the limp weight of the slightly-built girl.

'No, it's nobody's fault, my son!' a man took issue in a bass voice with the timbre of arrogant self-confidence often acquired by men of the cloth. 'After the Good Lord has ordained the time of our demise, then so it shall be!'

Edge briefly glanced at the tall, broadly-built, middle-aged man with a look of sanctimonious earnestness on his rugged-featured face. Then returned his attention to Christie. Felt he

123

should have something to say to the man who looked fixedly back at him still with an empty-eyed stare: seemed not to have heard what the preacher said.

He epitomised the complete greenhorn Easterner in these circumstances: freshly washed up and shaved, garbed in a neat suit not soiled and crumpled from the rigors of the long trail from Philadelphia. Looking helplessly lost: seeking comfort, condolence, advice or maybe just a simple explanation from an experienced Westerner so he might understand and come to terms with this eruption of Western violence that had culminated in the untimely death of the woman he loved. Or, at least, the woman for whom he had given up so much to be with.

But Edge could not begin to find the words—perhaps, he wondered, it was never in a man like him to discover the right words in such situations—before the double doors slammed closed.

And only the first part of what the enraged Mary Wilde yelled was heard outside: 'You're kind are no help at all, Daniel Lister! You ministers are all the same! The way you'd have us believe it's the will of the Almighty whatever evil calamity——'

The doors crashed together, but not before the group on the street glimpsed the shuddering sob that shook Christie's frame, was vented in a strangely muted sound compared with that jerking movement that quaked through him from head to toe.

Then came a harsh silence while the cluster of small-town men and women once more took time to reflect morosely on the latest violence that had come to their peaceful community. Ended when the minister attempted to justify his opinion.

'A complete understanding of the will of God is the foundation of Christian faith. Without such appreciation of how the Lord moves to perform his marvellous plan...'

Edge was among the first to turn away from the façade of the hotel, start back along the street where more bright lights than before shone out from store and house windows and doorways. None of them had the gleam of cheerfulness now.

And perhaps the brightest, yet the most forlorn, was the shaft of pale yellow that angled from the display window of the late Paul Smith's clothes store. A lot of people were inside the premises, but little noise emerged.

The many areas of lamplight illuminated small groups, couples and occasional lone individuals who mostly waited in downcast silence. Mourning the new dead, trying to recover from shock, watching as Harry Grimes and the posse gathered with their horses, mounted up and clattered out of town in the wake of the fugitives.

Vaughan Jameson and Ellen overhauled the ambling figure of the half-breed, would have hurried on past had not the small girl jerked her hand free of the man's grasp, slowed to match Edge's pace. She looked up at him with her dark, solemn eyes, said:

'Mister?'

'Young lady?' Edge peered down at her with the same degree of gravity she expressed.

'I want to thank you for getting my money back for me. The two dollars thirty seven cents I had saved up in Aunt Donna's bank?'

'Ellen, come along,' Jameson urged, showed a helpless frown to Edge.

'You're welcome,' the half-breed told the small girl. 'It's a shame it was stolen a second time.'

She nodded, replied guilelessly: 'Why aren't you going with Uncle Harry to help get everybody's money back again?'

'Ellen!' Jameson exploded. Nervousness made his voice squeakier than ever. Then something close to fear was in his eyes when he hurried to explain to Edge: 'I'm sorry. She's my niece, you know. My sister and her husband died in the big fever epidemic up around Denver last year. It's difficult for a bachelor to raise a girl of this age. But I'm Ellen's only kin.'

'No sweat, feller,' Edge told the man evenly as Jameson took a firm grip on the girl's hand, almost jerked her off her feet in his hurry to move away from the half-breed, headed for the row of houses across from the saloon. 'She asked a good question.'

His voice dropped to a murmur even though the gap to the

man and child had widened to several yards: 'One I don't have a good answer to.'

He stepped into the saloon where the sullen-faced John, in common with his diminished number of patrons, now had nothing at which to smile. He was supplying drinks to a handful of men, some of them needing liquid courage before they attended to the blood-stained body of David Doyle sprawled across the collapsed table.

The bottle Edge had left on the table in a rear corner was still there and when it was toward this table he was seen to go, John and the other customers paid him no further heed.

A little later, four men reluctantly carried the body of Doyle out of the saloon. Some indignant criticism was shrilly voiced by women in the street because they had not draped the corpse with a blanket. Then for several minutes after the men had returned, the sounds from outside gradually diminished. And there was little talk inside the Centennial, beyond monotoned requests for refills, terse demands for payment.

In this time, Edge nursed the single drink and smoked the one cigarette he had earlier thought about as a practical means to disassociate himself from the troubles of Munro. But he could not feel detached from it all: and with each quiet passing minute it even seemed he was developing a deeper, colder anger at what had happened since he rode into town yesterday.

Not out of empathy for Munro. Nor, he acknowledged now, did his stirred-up emotions have anything to do with sympathy for Conrad Christie. Or a sense of bereavement because of the violent end of Alice Brown. This couple who were instrumental in freeing him from the bunch of decrepit desperadoes at Eagle Rock last night: proving he was innocent of complicity in their crimes.

There were two other reasons: both of them selfish.

First, his pride still smarted because of how he allowed himself to get sucked into the whirlpool of ever-increasing violence by the mostly lame old men. Who treated him with the same degree of disdain as they held for the ordinary people of this country town: who had no occasion, and

126

therefore no need, to be able to handle themselves in this kind of murderous trouble.

Second — and it was not for the first time he had been plagued by this kind of nagging doubt—although he was anxious to emulate Steele, if ever he found the Virginian had successfully broken away from the drifting life of a saddle-tramp, he knew it was not possible for a man to turn his back entirely on other people's misery. Trials and tribulations, damnit, embodied by the helplessness of a nine-year-old orphan girl robbed of her few cents savings.

A state of perfection certainly did not exist anywhere in this world: north or south of any border. And if he truly aspired to attain something as close as it was possible to find on this imperfect earth, he would have to be ready to fight for it, take a hand in keeping things that way.

Right now, maybe, he could stroll on down the street to the livery, get his horse and gear out, turn his back on and ride away from what was happening here in Munro. But what if such violence had erupted in a place that attracted him as much as the Providence River Valley appealed to Adam Steele?

'A man like you, he should've ridden along with the posse and helped them.'

Edge did not need to check the level of the whiskey in the bottle to know he had not drunk more than one extra shot since he returned to the Centennial Saloon. So he knew he was not imagining a censuring voice of conscience making itself heard in the forefront of his mind.

'Or are you the kind of man who only does that kind of man-hunting chore if there's bounty money to be had for it?'

He looked up at the two of them. The first to speak had been the big and broad, blonde or maybe white haired Clara Cornwall. There was an unladylike grimace on her less than handsome features, but dressed all in black she looked a lot more feminine than in the dungarees and work boots she was wearing when he saw her at the bank yesterday and early this morning when he gave her an opportunity to kill him with his own gun.

His stomach knotted at the memory of that moment of idiocy.

The younger, easier-on-the-eye Laura Grimes had forgotten to take off her grease-stained and flour-powdered waist apron after the violent interruption to the evening kitchen chores. She eyed Edge with a kind of weary contempt: like maybe she had started to think better of him at some time during the day, but now was bitterly disappointed.

Their surprise entry into the saloon and what they had said to the half-breed had brought a brittle silence to the place as they stood before his table like a two-woman deputation.

Again he did not stand in female company but he did straighten up from where he had slumped a little in the chair while he contemplated the very subject they had just raised. He invited 'You want to sit down, ladies?'

'I don't indulge in strong drink, and I'm sure neither does Mrs Cornwall,' Laura Grimes answered frostily.

For a moment or two the older woman looked uneasy and Edge guessed she was not strictly an abstainer. He said:

'I was inviting you to sit down at my table, not to drink with me, ma'am.'

This drew a blushing startled look from the younger woman.

The older one glowered around at the half dozen customers still left in the saloon, then accused them harshly: 'And I should think you men would've somethin' better to do tonight. Except drink yourselves into stupors in this dreadful place!'

The bartender snarled: 'When you've finished tryin' to empty my saloon of regular customers, be real obliged if you two Carry Nations will get the hell out yourselves! I got a livin' to make here!'

When Edge heard the harsh tone of the man's voice, he knew it was the same John who had been so vocally aggressive toward him in the wake of the bank robbery yesterday afternoon. If it mattered. He was still not sure if anything about this town and its troubles mattered to him.

'Hush up, Clara,' Laura Grimes urged. She looked quickly around the dimly lit, smoke-and liquor-reeking room:

128

seemed to become aware of her unsavoury and unfamiliar
surroundings for the first time and was a little afraid of them.
Like a child in a lonely wood when she sees it is getting dark.

Then she asked diffidently of the bartender: 'Please, Mr
Bruce. Do you have sarsaparilla? Or milk, anything like that?'

'I got plenty of sarsaparilla for little kids that wait outside
for their Pas, Mrs Grimes.' With his expression and tone he
endeavoured to make the response into an insult.

'Two glasses, please.' She returned her attention to Edge.
'We'll accept your invitation to share your table, Mr Edge.
Naturally, we'll pay for our own drinks. Here, Clara: sit.'

She drew out a chair, held it and waited until the scowling
older woman was seated before she sat down herself: like she
was worried Mrs Cornwall might make a dash for the door,
or launch an attack on one of the disgruntled men. And she
would not be able to stop it unless she were on her feet. Then
she promised:

'We'll come directly to the point.'

A man mumbled: 'For a woman, that's impossible.'

Another man spat, scored a moist direct hit into a spittoon.

Edge recorked the bottle deliberately. Dropped his
cigarette butt on the floor and ground out the glowing ash
under a heel, said: 'That's fine, ma'am. Always been a better
listener than a talker. But I can lose interest fast if the point's a
long time coming.'

'A man of few words, less patience and hardly any manners
at all!' Clara Cornwall growled and Edge thought she was
trying to strike back at him because of how he had called her
bluff this morning.

'I made no claims about manners, lady,' he said.

The younger woman hurried to get to the purpose of their
visit. 'Harry... my husband... the sheriff: he asked me to
speak with you, Mr Edge. Just before he led the posse on the
heels of those wanton murderers.'

Mrs Cornwall said: 'I'm along because Laura thought she
needed support in this revolting place, and I can't say I'm
surprised.'

John Bruce took the trouble to bring the two glasses of
fizzing liquid to the table. He set them down with calculated

decorum, then looked bleakly at each woman in turn as he growled: 'On the house, ladies. Just to show you didn't oughta cock your snoots at everythin' about my place.'

'Your generosity's exceeded only by your beauty, John!' an elderly man called. His cackle of thin laughter triggered a ripple of amusement from the other patrons.

Without turning around Clara Cornwall accused coldly: 'I suppose, Solomon Gerber, you'll figure makin' jokes is right when your drinkin' finally drives that poor wife of yours into her grave?'

Somebody said meekly: 'She's right, Sol.'

'Yeah, real sorry about Nicky, Clara,' Gerber offered contritely.

'And don't forget so quickly Mr Smith and David Doyle. Or the poor young woman who——'

'All right, you've made your point, Clara,' Laura broke in. Allowed a pause to see if the gloomy silence would hold long enough to satisfy the grieving older woman. Then, peering levelly at the half-breed: 'In the event you leave town before Harry returns, Mr Edge, he asked me to ask you what you meant about being able to help? When you plainly did not intend to join the posse?'

A couple of the men, indifferent to the question and answer, began to talk softly with their heads close together. But the rest seemed to listen while they tried to make out they did not.

Edge eyed the two women for several moments. Saw the grief just under the veneer of Clara Cornwall's toughness, and undisguised eager interest mixed with the insecure bitterness Laura Grimes tried to project. Decided he might just as well get it said here and now. For it was quite probable he would have left Munro before the posse rode back into town.

'All I've got is a list of names. Maybe they'll mean something to people around here?'

'We're listening,' Laura invited, even showed the trace of a fleeting smile.

Clara leaned forward, and now everyone else in the Centennial was suddenly as avidly attentive as the women.

'Ruben Banning. Eugene Miller. Richard Shelby. Edward

130

Duffy—they call him Duff. And Pete Race.'

Laura looked crestfallen, sounded even more so when she responded: 'Race was the man Mr Parker shot after yesterday's bank hold up. Miss Terry mentioned some of the given names you just did. So I presume they're the men who robbed the bank and did the killing?'

'Right.'

'They don't mean anything around here,' Clara Cornwall said adamantly. 'Far as I know.' She shrugged her broad shoulders and looked about her. 'Any of our people ever heard of——'

'Just that guy Race Sam Parker plugged,' the old-timer who shared a table with Gerber said. 'Killed him in the end, I heard. Ain't that so, mister?'

'He bled to death of the wound, feller.'

Clara Cornwall tried to look pleased at the image. Laura Grimes shuddered.

'Anyway,' John Bruce growled. 'If any of them were known around here, we'd have spotted them yesterday. Stupid bast... crazy old fools were in here drinkin' beer before they went out and put on them masks to hit the bank.'

'How about a feller called Charlie?' Edge asked. 'He had nothing to do with yesterday's hold up. Heard it said that what happened to Race was more or less the same thing that happened to Charlie. Awhile ago, maybe?'

'Charlie's a pretty widespread kind of name, mister,' Bruce pointed out. 'We got three of them right here in Munro.'

'And not one of them fellers would have anythin' to do with——' Mrs Cornwall started to argue.

Edge went on, addressing Laura Grimes: 'The feller who brought up the name Charlie was shut up fast by the others. Like it was a big secret I shouldn't hear about.'

This heralded a brief silence, until:

'That it?' Clara Cornwall asked, and sounded scornful of all she had heard.

'Just the one more thing. The old-timers figured they had a good reason for hitting the bank here in Munro. Like they had a grudge to settle: call to hate this town.'

The two women looked at each other, puzzled. Then rose,

looked down at Edge like they wished they could press him for more information: details that meant something to them.

'That's everything I had to tell the sheriff, ladies,' Edge said. 'Knew the men were seen drinking in here, so they couldn't be recognised. But maybe that was because a lot of years have gone by since they would've been. If the names don't register...' He shrugged.

The two women turned away, Clara with a low grunt of disgust, Laura wearing something akin to a kind of consoling smile: almost like she felt Edge might be as disappointed as they were at how the conversation had failed to produce positive results. And he recalled what Harry Grimes had said about his wife of a few months who considered she also had a mother role to play.

'Thank you so much for the drinks, Mr Bruce,' the younger woman said. 'Since we did not touch them perhaps we should offer to pay?'

'Thanks, but no thanks, lady,' the sullen-faced bartender said suddenly. 'Be payment enough far as I'm concerned if the two of you don't ever come in the Centennial again.'

'There is no chance we will, that's for sure!' Clara said as she pushed open one of the batwings, held it for the younger woman to go out of the saloon ahead of her.

'Shit! I know!' Solomon Gerber blurted.

'Watch your filthy tongue in the presence of——' the older woman began to snarl, but then her voice faded away as she peered fixedly at the grey-haired, thin-faced, watery-eyed old man who unfolded upright from his chair so violently he knocked it over backwards. And it was obvious he had vented a vocal reaction to a startling thought without any intention of offending anyone.

'What is it, Mr Gerber?' Laura asked anxiously. 'Has something Mr Edge said reminded you of——'

'Charlie, Mrs Grimes! I reckon it could've been Charlie Riley the old boys was meanin'.'

'Who's Charlie Riley?' Bruce demanded. He scowled at the old man who was suddenly at the centre of attention. Like he was used to Gerber causing a disturbance in his saloon and had grown weary of it. 'Ain't nobody in Munro with that name.'

132

'Sure there is,' the man he shared the table with said happily, a grin breaking out across his hollow-eyed, prominently-cheekboned, unshaven face. Plainly was pleased he had been able to call to mind the same memory as the man who stood across the table from him.

Gerber said: 'In the cemetery.'

'Only it don't say nothin' on his grave about who's buried there, right Sol?'

'Right, Virgil.'

'Just what is all this about?' Laura Grimes asked, swallowed nervously as she looked anxiously about the saloon.

Clara Cornwall released the batwing so it flapped closed across half the entrance, met with the other one. She demanded: 'Well, what are you gettin' at, Solomon? Spit it out now!'

'Yeah, you got yourself an audience, the way you like to,' Bruce growled.

Gerber's attitude became earnest as he righted the chair, carefully sat down on it, said with a series of slow nods: 'Spit it out? Yeah, that's just the right way to put it, Clara. Spit is what folks usually do if they got themselves a bad taste in the mouth, ain't it?'

Laura urged anxiously: 'Mr Gerber?'

'Yeah, quit yakkin' around in circles, you damned old fool!' Bruce complained sourly.

There was a ripple of mumbled agreement within the saloon. Then Gerber looked down into his almost empty shot glass which he held in both hands, said:

'We never used to put names on the graves of men we strung up. Right, Virgil?'

'Yep. Sometimes never even knew the names of some of the sonsofbitches—excuse me, ladies—who we strung up back in them days.'

Laura gasped: 'You mean the people of this town once——'

'From the old oak tree used to grow out back of the Grand Hotel, Mrs Grimes,' Virgil confirmed, nodded emphatically.

Laura pressed: 'Without a trial to find out if they were guilty?'

'Yep. There were a whole lotta lynchin's in Munro in them days, right Sol?'

'Sure was. 'Course, it wasn't the same town way back then. Wasn't the same country, this far west of the Mississippi.'

'Oh, my goodness!' Laura gasped, needed to support her swaying form with a hand splayed against the wall near the doorway.

Virgil vented a short, ruthless laugh, finished the heeltaps in his glass, said: 'Used to call the occasions necktie parties. They were real wild, them kinda shindigs. Weren't never over until some guy was sent for the last drop.'

15

Laura made a sound as if, in a very ladylike way, she was struggling to keep herself from being sick to her stomach. And now Clara held a chair for the younger woman, steered her into sitting on it. Then pointedly ignored the foolishly grinning Virgil to ask coldly of Gerber:

'How long ago did this happen? I don't remember nothin' about Munro ever bein' the kind of town went in for that kind of rough justice. And I been here best part of thirty years.'

Gerber had not shared in Virgil's black humour, was sedately pensive when he asked: 'What year we in now, Clara?'

It was John Bruce who told him.

Gerber made a calculation, needed to use his bony fingers to check it. Finally concluded, as Virgil looked at him as earnestly as anyone else: 'Forty six . . . No, it's October now, ain't it? Be forty seven years ago we hung Charlie Riley.'

He was still frowning from the effort of delving into the long-ago past when he peered over the length of the saloon toward Edge, asked: 'You reckon it could be the Charlie Riley—the last man who ever got strung up in Munro— who's the one them old boys were meanin', mister? It was a Saturday night, as I recall.'

'More like early Sunday mornin',' Virgil corrected.

'That's hardly important, Mr Snyder,' Laura said.

Edge asked: 'Was he a young feller?'

Virgil, eager to do some of the telling, said: 'Little more'n twenty: twenty one or two, maybe. Same as Sol and me were back then.'

Gerber nodded his agreement.

Edge said: 'If it means anything, I'd say Riley was in the same age group as the bunch who robbed the bank. Forty seven years ago they'd all have been about twenty or so.'

'So by a stretch of the imagination, perhaps...' Laura started, shuddered.

Virgil vented another of his terse laughs. 'Wasn't his imagination we stretched way back then, was his——'

'Shut up, Virgil,' Solomon Gerber said, irritated and embarrassed by his friend's ill-placed humour.

'Yeah, shut up, Virgil Snyder, now we're startin' to get somewhere,' Clara snarled. And for the first time showed a sign of excitement through her cynicism about the wisdom of this whole interlude in the Centennial Saloon. 'I suppose, Solomon, the people of the town lynched Riley for some crime or other?'

Laura Grimes shuddered, peered at the doorway beyond which the silent, empty street was ghostly dark. 'I just can't contemplate people here doin——'

'Guess that's why I fastened on the name so easy, Clara,' Gerber said. 'It was the same kinda crime. See, Riley and five other trigger-happy kids robbed the town bank, shot the man who run it. Feller called... Hell, I don't even remember his name now.'

'Edward Arbuthnot, Sol,' Virgil supplied. Solemn faced, eager to re-establish his credibility as a source of information. 'Yep, it's kinda like history repeatin' itself, ain't it? When you come to think of it?'

Somebody pointed out: 'Well, Edge here did say as how the Race guy cashin' in his chips was kinda like what happened to Charlie.'

The half-breed rose from his corner table and the move drew the attention of everyone as he came to the bar counter with the bottle. He said to the bartender:

'Four shots. Forty cents, right?'

Bruce nodded indifferently without a glance at the level of liquor in the bottle, then like everyone else peered at the table where Gerber and Snyder sat.

There was some low-toned talk as Edge countered out coins to cover his tab: intended to leave the Centennial, get some supper, then decide whether to bed down for the night at the Grand Hotel or head right on out. But doubted he could sleep so soon after spending all day in bed, and he was not so hungry as he had been.

The other people in the saloon moved closer to the table shared by the pair of old men at the centre of intrigued and horrified attention. Even John Bruce came out from behind his counter to join the converging audience. Brought with him a bottle after Gerber had made it unsubtly clear he would like a refill of his glass and Laura Grimes promised she would pay for drinks for Gerber and Snyder.

Then Edge found himself held there at the counter: rolled and smoked a cigarette as he listened to the full story of the lynching. Told by Solomon Gerber, interrupted by Virgil Snyder from time to time with details Gerber had forgotten or corrections to errors that were usually unimportant.

But the story emerged lucidly, in a way that could be clearly understood by all those who heard it in the dimly lit saloon; the atmosphere growing colder and less malodorous as the stove was allowed to go out, and night air flowed in under and over the batwings to neutralise the smells of unwashed bodies, burning tobacco and fresh-poured liquor.

Forty-seven years ago Munro was little more than a once prosperous mining camp, but it was starting to become a stopover town on the stage line between Denver and points east and San Francisco. The only stone building on the then unnamed main street was the newly constructed Grand Hotel: run by the grandfather of Mary Eastwood who would arrive later, just widowed as Mary Wilde, to inherit the place. The local bank had no name or affiliation with any others in those days. It was run by Edward Arbuthnot from a wooden shack about where Paul Smith's clothing store now stood.

There was still some silver being unearthed on scattered claims, and most of the grubbers kept their finds in the bank. Along with whatever money they had from selling nuggets: whatever money, anyway, they did not spend in the Lucky Cartwheel Saloon—which was where the livery stables were now—and a house of ill-repute known as Annie's Place. This had been at the other end of the street: about where the schoolhouse stood today.

A church, since rebuilt, and the cemetery, had always been

137

where they were.

There was often disagreement between the two old-timers about geographical references, and at first some of the listeners were irritably impatient about these inconsequentials. But they soon realised it was easier just to put up with the pace set by Gerber and Snyder. Allowed the old men to sidetrack without complaint now and then to draw out the pertinent details of that other lethal bank robbery and its brutal aftermath almost a half century ago.

The six young men wearing kerchief masks over their lower faces galloped their horses into the small community in the middle of a hot and dusty Wednesday afternoon. Hit the bank, and when Arbuthnot attempted to protect the safe, shot him in the head.

When they raced out of town, shooting wildly and yelling like liquor-crazed Indians, one of the six had his horse shot out from under him. He was almost lynched there and then in this frontier town at a time when the rule of civilised law counted for little. But reason prevailed: he was just one of a six-man gang who killed Arbuthnot and he didn't have any of the money taken from the bank.

Neither Gerber nor Snyder made any claims about being for or against the call for instant justice: nor to having a hand in cooling the situation down.

They remembered the names of some men, had forgotten many others: all of them long gone from Munro, most of them certainly dead of old age if nothing else. The leaders of the community in those days held a meeting in the Lucky Cartwheel where it was decided not to treat Riley like a common horsethief, a claim jumper, a fast gun who shot the wrong man or a pervert harassing a woman who did not work at Annie's Place.

So Riley was locked in the dugout which back then served as a jail, a guard mounted on him, to wait and see if his partners tried to free him.

It was at this point of the account Virgil Snyder made a valid interruption. Recalled Riley had started the line of thinking: claimed he and his buddies never allowed one of their own to stay in jail for long. It had been like that all the way from Chicago where they had started out on so many stealing trails along which they hit stages, trains, banks, stores, farms and ranches: any man who got captured was always busted out real soon.

Laura Grimes thought to prod the memories of Gerber and Snyder for names, but neither of them could recall if any were mentioned to match those Edge had listed.

Then Clara asked: 'The friends of Riley never came for him, so he was lynched? That what happened?'

'No, no it didn't, lady,' Virgil was quick to contradict. 'Tell her, Sol.'

'They came all right, Clara. Two of them under a flag of truce. Wearing masks again, just like them guys hit Miss Terry's bank two times now. There was some dickerin' and they was told to hand over the stolen money and goods in exchange for Riley: us folks would go for a deal like that. So that's the arrangements were made.'

'Trade-off was gonna be on the Sunday mornin', right Sol?'

'Yeah, the Sunday mornin'. Along at the west end of the street, outside Annie's Place. But Saturday night a whole lotta drinkin' went on. Same happened every Saturday night. At the Lucky Cartwheel and at Annie's Place.

'Things were different in them days: folks thought different. But things were startin' to change. Stuck in a lot of folks' craws, that what happened to Arbuthnot—him gettin' shot in the head like he did—wasn't gonna count for nothin'. Long as them with cash and goods in the bank got back what was theirs.'

'Me and Sol didn't have nothin' in the bank to get back,' Virgil interjected, and was ignored.

Gerber went on: 'Bunch of us, we went to the hole-in-the-ground jail.'

'About where old Sam Parker's house is these days.'

'Dragged Riley outta there. Hauled his screamin' ass... took him over to the Grand Hotel, out to the oak in the backyard. A lot were against it, but most were for it: and wasn't gonna be stopped. Strung him up. Used a wagon, with a bunch of guys to jerk it out from under him.'

Again Gerber and Snyder did not say which side of the

argument they had favoured.

Laura Grimes vented a muted sound, almost like a stifled howl.

'Next mornin', we waited for the rest of the gang to show up with the money and stuff. Was ready to round them up, shoot them down if that was how they wanted it. But they didn't come. Not all of them, not one of them. Must've been watchin', seen what we done in the night. Knew we didn't have nothin' left to trade with. For awhile after that, a whole lotta folks didn't sleep easy in their beds. Didn't like to move too far away from other people. Fearful of revenge, I guess. But it never come.'

'Until yesterday and tonight, maybe,' a man muttered.

'Could be,' Bruce growled. 'Forty-seven years, that's a lot of time to carry a grudge.'

'Riley was the last man ever to be lynched in Munro,' Virgil added. 'I think they even cut down the old oak pretty soon afterwards, didn't they, Sol?'

'Yeah, just a couple of weeks later, I think,' Gerber agreed grimly. 'Wonder how many other folks can recall all of that, Virgil? I can't think of anyone still left around here, can you?'

'Except them buried in the cemetery same as Riley, Sol.'

'Dead men didn't remember nothin', Virgil. Nor tell no tales. Guess it's lucky you and me are still here to help these folks, uh?'

'Trouble is,' Clara Cornwall growled as she rose slowly to her feet, rubbed the corners of her eyes with a finger and thumb like the time and the talk in the saloon had wearied her, 'it ain't been no help at all. Except it makes sense of somethin' Edge overheard. Which don't make no difference to bringin' the killers of my Nicky and the others to justice.'

'That surely is right,' Laura Grimes agreed dejectedly as she unfolded from her chair. This time reached the batwings first, held open a door for the older woman to leave ahead of her.

Edge pushed away from the bar counter as the rest of the group at the table dispersed: Bruce to return to his bar and the other four customers to their own tables. While Solomon Gerber and Virgil Snyder stayed put, maybe the only ones aware they had acquired a free bottle of whiskey Laura

Grimes had not gotten around to paying for.

'That's some can of worms you opened up, uh?' Bruce asked of Edge. 'Forty-seven years old.'

Clara Cornwall paused in the doorway and asked: 'But what does it matter? Unless the sheriff and his posse can find the killers, the lid goes right back on. A bunch of names isn't any use unless you have the addresses to go with them.'

Edge stepped out of the saloon in the wake of the two women, dropped his cigarette butt to the ground, put out its fire under a heel as he watched them cross the street, angling away from each other toward the houses where they lived.

He heard Laura say in a tremulous voice: 'I don't think I'll ever be able to walk past Mary Wilde's place without thinking about all those men who were hanged without trial out back of it.'

'That's all we're left with, my dear,' Clara answered, sounding as drained as she looked. 'Ghosts of the long dead and some meaningless names. It's not much. Even the tree was chopped down.'

Edge spat between his feet and the sound caused the two to snap their heads around, look at him over their shoulders. He tipped his hat, said:

'I'm sorry I disappointed you ladies. Guess in this case great oaks from little acorns won't grow.'

16

Edge ate alone in the neat, clean, stove-heated dining room of the Grand Hotel. Delicious pot roast with the trimmings that Mary Wilde had asked if he wouldn't mind helping himself to: the black would take care of clearing up after him.

Then she and Conrad Christie had resumed some kind of cultured wake they were holding in the parlour. Without the body of Alice Brown which had been taken away from the hotel to be placed with the remains of Nicky Cornwall, Paul Smith and David Doyle in the church to await burial.

Because the hotel and the cemetery were almost at opposite ends of Lark Street, while the half-breed ate supper he could not hear the sounds of the graves being dug ready for the corpses to be interred in a mass funeral the next morning.

The chore was completed by the time he stepped out of the hotel, after leaving the cost of a day's stay and the two meals on the table in the dining room.

At the livery he left what he considered a fair price for having his gelding stabled, watered and fed for the thirty-plus hours since the horse was taken into the care of David Doyle. He placed this money under an empty coffee pot on the cold stove in the livery: neither knowing nor caring who would get the cash. David Doyle sure couldn't collect, but Edge was satisfied in his own mind he had paid his way in this town.

He was also content he had paid his dues to the town as a whole: felt a degree of gratitude to the two women for having persuaded him to tell what he knew: so he did not have to decide if he should wait until the posse returned.

As far as he knew, he was not seen nor heard leaving the quiet, darkened town—only a dim light gleamed in the hotel parlour—at something after midnight. Certainly he had no feeling of being watched as he rode slowly out to the west. But that did not necessarily mean his leaving went unnoticed. Just that anyone who observed him did not feel hostility toward him.

He smelled the fresh-turned earth of the four newly-dug graves as he passed the cemetery with the church where the dead lay in the rear corner of the walled enclosure.

Recalled as he glanced to the other side of the street the way a woman had sung cheerfully, had been ready to welcome strangers to town yesterday morning. Before she was provoked to running scared into her house when she saw who was driving the Christies' Conestoga.

At least, though, the situation had altered since then. Munro was now a town he could leave without rancour or contempt following him. Not his town: but if he ever came upon a community where he thought he might belong, he could consider he had started to learn the lessons of how to respond to the people of such a community. How to take a hand on the periphery of their problems without the embittered feeling he had been trapped into taking such actions by his malevolent ruling fates.

He never met up with the Munro posse as he angled southward from town, then swung west on the trail that later forked at Eagle Rock and its long abandoned stage line way station. Never saw anyone for many days that lengthened into more than two weeks as he continued to ride westward, navigating by the sun during the day after the trail petered out, sleeping soundly at nights.

He had not attempted to track sign from the outset, sought it only from habit: in the event marauders—Indian or white—be laying in ambush for him, to kill him for his horse and gear.

He was many miles over the Colorado state line into the Territory of Utah or maybe had drifted far enough south to have crossed into the north of Arizona when he began to see he did not have the whole of the southern Rockies to himself.

First, far off his elected route, he glimpsed the smoke of small camp or stove fires. Later spotted in the distance the clustered buildings of isolated farmstead or ranches. Next saw spur trails that came down out of the hills. Finally reached the point where these spurs came together at the start of a main, more heavily used trail.

This at an element-worn and time-ravaged dirt farm where a couple named Grossman, younger than they looked, and their two sons in the middle teen years regarded him with undisguised suspicion, but eagerly sold him some supplies: were obviously glad to see him leave with directions to a town called Pomona, fifteen miles to the west. Where he could maybe buy better, but not so cheap, they claimed dejectedly.

It was late afternoon when he left the depressed Grossman place, and he covered about half the distance to town before he bedded down beside the trail. In the night his sleep was briefly disturbed by the distant hoofbeats of a fast-ridden horse, the rider far to the south of where he was camped: heading east to west.

He awoke at the bright, cold dawn the next morning, cooked up a better breakfast of fresher food than he had eaten since he left Munro. And then as he broke camp he saw a rider to the south, heading west to east at a less frenetic pace than the one in the night. Surely the same one?

He reached Pomona at mid-morning, having ridden by a number of other farmsteads, less isolated than the Grossman place. Where, perhaps because he did not pause, he was sometimes welcomed with vigorous waves and shouted greetings. But those who saw him at close quarters were less demonstrative.

Pomona looked to be about the same population size as Munro. More strung out along its main street that looped around a timber-encircled sink hole that was doubtless the reason a community was sited at this point in the mountains.

A town limits marker, almost fallen down, proclaimed *Welcome to Pomona*, and under this in smaller lettering boasted *Sweetest Water in the Territory*. Edge had to rein his gelding to a halt, peer long and hard to read the claim on the leaning sign. It was a long time since the marker was painted: maybe it never had been repainted.

Starting along the street that curved slightly to the south and sloped down a shallow gradient to skirt the sink hole at a midway point, he saw the sign was representative of the less

144

than spick and span condition of the town.

Pomona was comprised entirely of unimposing single story timber buildings which had withstood the worst of the mountain elements and attrition of the passing years without collapsing. But the people who tended them had done only what was strictly necessary to keep the roofs free of holes and the walls from caving in. No one had lavished too much time and effort on non-essential decorative maintenance. So there was a depressingly threadbare aspect to the town.

When he rode past the small clapboard church with peeling and bubbled white paintwork he did not fail to see a recent grave, the wreaths of flowers, dead for two weeks or so, on the dirt mound.

The new grave fitted in with the rider in the night: and early morning.

From more than two hundred yards away as he advanced at an even pace down the sloping and curving street, knew he was viewed with much the same kind of suspicion he attracted when he first showed in any small town, the planks of newly sawn lumber piled directly across the street from the sink hole appeared fresh and clean looking in such dilapidated surroundings. Even seen through the distorting haze of smoke and heat shimmer that rose from a smouldering fire on the site of a former building recently consumed by much fiercer flames.

There was a sprinkling of people on the street which had no roofed sidewalks: here and there a run of boards laid directly on to the hard-packed ground outside the occasional store. Some offered tacit greetings less bright than the sun. Most were as coldly disposed toward the Stetson-hatted, sheep-skin-coated rider as the morning air.

The closer he got to the centre of town the fewer people were to be seen.

Then the suspicion aroused by the night rider and the new grave in the Pomona churchyard along with the attitudes of the local people produced the inevitable positive result. He experienced a familiar sensation that something was wrong. Which was immediately confirmed when he glanced over each shoulder in turn, saw those people who had greeted him with fleeting smiles or eyed him with silent mistrust had vanished off the street, withdrawn into the flanking buildings.

No voices had been raised, nor signs given that he had seen—and he would have seen, he was sure. But this was an isolated country town in the kind of territory that had once been dangerous: apparently still could be. And the people who lived their close-knit lives in Pomona were gifted by experience with the same kind of mysterious instinct for danger such as herd animals invariably possessed. Could sniff the unmoving air and detect the threat of impending violence, the faintly saline scent of blood before it is spilled. Silently communicate their findings to each other.

Edge commanded something of the same brand of instinct, but he could smell only the acrid taint of smoke after he could hear only the crackle of dying flames on the almost burnt-out fire competing with the clop of his mount's hooves.

Until, from a line of three small houses to his left, two larger ones on the right, there came the sound of doors and windows creaking open, repeater rifles being pumped, revolver hammers cocked. As many pairs of lungs were voided of pent up breath.

He reined in his mount, became rigid and ready for fast reaction to sudden attack behind the apparently casual attitude he maintained in his saddle. This as he saw a familiar figure appear at the open doorway of the nearest of a line of stores just beyond the fire-razed building where a small fire smouldered, the new timber was stacked, some sixty feet away.

'Howdy, Mr Edge,' the thin-bodied, fleshy-faced Ruben Banning called. He lifted his stick—a new, full length malacca cane—in greeting.

The short, heavily-built Edward Duffy, stiff-legged Richard Shelby and bespectacled Eugene Miller filed out behind Banning. Two of them held steaming cups: Duffy had two, one of which he gave to Banning. All four old-timers wore battered hats, dungarees, check shirts and work boots. And from a distance all of them looked like hick uncles.

Shelby said in a challenging tone that totally lacked warmth: 'Be about a dozen guns coverin' you, mister! So you

146

wanna give our friends and neighbours—some of our kin—that warnin' you always give folks that aim guns at you?'

'Aw now, hush up, Rich,' Banning censured in his avuncular manner. 'We have no call to provoke Mr Edge. No reason at all to get off on an unfriendly footing here in our own home town.'

'Right happy to be friends with him, Rube,' Duffy said with a gap-toothed grin, his tone almost as easy as that of Banning. Except there was just a slight inflection that hinted at latent sarcasm. 'Just so long as he don't go on again like my Aunt Rosina's parrot about his hundred and fif——'

'Someone from the Grossman farm warned you I was coming this way, uh?' Edge cut in on Duffy, looked at the man with the shiny black cane.

'Barny Grossman's younger boy rode into town to say a man like the one we described was heading on in, Edge,' Banning answered. 'So we made a few preparations. Would you like to stop by Duff's store here, sit a spell? Talk over old times?' The smile slipped off his face as he added, tone abruptly hard: 'How they affect the present?'

'Sure,' Edge said, heeled his horse forward and felt easier inside as he sensed a lessening of tension in the flanking houses. Even though he knew some gun muzzles continued to track his progress. Guessed the ordinary people of Pomona were considerably relieved he had not caused the trouble they had been led to expect. Now was becoming the problem of the quartet of old-timers out front of the store which Edge was now close enough to see had a sign running across the door and flanking display windows: *Duffy's Grocery*.

Having seen this, he looked at other business premises on the more sharply curved length of street that rose beyond the tree-encircled sink hole. Saw *Daniel Banning's Livery, Race Meat Market, Betta Shelby's Bakery, Miller's Dry Goods*. Last of all, a brand new sign, lettered white with gold edging on a black background, that had still to be erected on a building not yet constructed. It leaned against the stack of new timber, proclaimed: *The Charles K. Riley Elementary School*.

As he halted his horse out front of the grocery he saw for

the first time that none of the old men was visibly armed. Close to, the steam rising from the coffee in their cups smelled of liquor.

'You said the money was intended for a good cause, feller,' Edge said as he shifted his gaze from the sign to the group of men after he swung out of the saddle.

'Old school burned down,' Miller explained unnecessarily.

'Just burnin' up the last of the debris of the fire,' Shelby added.

Duffy said: 'That one didn't have no name.'

'You'll come inside, Edge?' Banning asked. 'Have a cup of coffee? With a little somethin' added, if you've a mind? Discover what it has all been about?'

'Unless you already know it from talkin' with Munro folks?' Duffy asked.

'They couldn't know so——' Miller started.

Banning interrupted: 'He could only have heard part of the story.'

'Right, feller. And a little learning can be a dangerous thing, uh?'

Shelby scowled as he warned: 'Let's hope nobody has to teach nobody else any hard lessons.'

Edge looped his reins around a hitching post, said: 'Education is a wonderful thing: figure we all subscribe to that school of thought.'

17

Edward Duffy kept a clean, well-stocked grocery store. A counter ran along the rear and one side wall. There were floor to ceiling shelves behind the counter, a row of loose-topped barrels and bulging sacks in back of the display windows. Five chairs were arranged in a half circle around the pot-bellied stove that was backed against the centre of the other side wall.

The warmth of the stove was a minor luxury after the chill bite of the bright morning air. And the aromatic mixture of coffee, liquor and some of the grocery stock was just as welcome after the acrid taint of old and new burning outside.

There was fresh-made coffee in the pot on the hot stove and a cup was filled by Miller, the steam misting his eyeglasses as he handed it to Edge. Banning directed the half-breed to take one of the two chairs closest to the stove: that nearest to the rear of the store.

The normal sounds of a small, unbustling town at mid-morning had started to drift in through the open doorway when Edge told Duffy, who reached for a bottle on the nearby rear counter, he never drank hard liquor before noon.

'How'd you know where to find us?' Shelby demanded harshly as soon as they were all seated in the mismatched ladderbacks.

'I didn't, feller.'

'Uh?' The slitted eyes of Shelby glinted irritably.

Banning nodded, scratched his almost bald head in the horseshoe of grey hair, showed a satisfied smile. 'A man who just happens to stumble across something when he isn't actually looking for it cannot be said to have found what he is looking for, Rich.'

'Heading for California and——'

Shelby, who sat immediately next to Edge, cut in: 'There's a stage trail through Munro. Goes all the way out to San Francisco, mister. Been a lot easier to ride that trail.'

'San Francisco's not where I'm headed in California, feller,' Edge told Shelby, then peered at Banning who sat directly opposite him in the chair at the far end of the arching line. 'Didn't even know there was a town here before I reached the Grossman place. And until I heard somebody riding this way in the night, spotted him go on back home this morning then saw the new grave in the local cemetery, I had no reason to count on you fellers being here.'

Duffy sat next to Shelby. He said: nodding slowly: 'Pete's grave. What about other Munro people? The sheriff and a posse, maybe?'

'They were still out trying to pick up on your tracks when I left town,' Edge answered, set his cup on the floor, dug out the makings.

'It don't matter so much, seems to me,' Miller said, his voice sounding croakier than usual when he was thoughtful. 'He's here on his own. If there's a bunch of guys with tin stars on their chests headin' in, we'll get the word: same as we did about him.'

Banning vented a deep, long sigh, rapped the ferrule of his new cane on the clean floor, complained: 'Buddies, we're sounding more like a gaggle of nervous old women instead of the bunch of desperadoes Edge said we were, uh?'

'Been a long time since we ever were that, really,' Eugene Miller muttered dejectedly.

Banning peered fixedly at Edge, said: 'And we don't ever have to try to be again. Now that old score has been settled: although that wasn't our prime objective, you understand? What did you hear in Munro, Mr Edge?'

The half-breed took the time to light his cigarette, then tossed the dead match in the hearth fronting the stove, picked up his cup of coffee before he asked: 'What happened there forty-seven years ago. On a hot Wednesday afternoon. Then a drunken Saturday night: or maybe that was late enough to be the Sunday morning.'

Shelby made a throaty sound like he was not pleased he

had been proved right about something, then muttered: 'It was gone midnight.'

Miller said with a strangely sad shake of his head: 'So there's still an old guy alive and kickin' who was there? Maybe had a hand in what happened to Charlie?'

'Two.'

Banning pointed out: 'Five . . . four of us are left. It always figured there'd be some of the old people still in that town.' He paused briefly for reflective thought. Then spoke in a more determined tone. 'But, of course, that wasn't why we wore the masks, Edge. We didn't at first. Not when we rode in, went into the saloon before we held up the bank. We only then decided on the masks. I suppose it was for old time's sake.'

'When we were really desperadoes,' Duffy said ruefully. 'Robbin' trains and stages and banks in the old days.'

'Right,' Banning agreed. 'But that all ended soon after we were cheated so tragically by the people of Munro. Who lynched Charlie Riley when they'd made a deal to exchange him for what we stole from the town bank.'

'We'd have honoured the deal,' Miller assured earnestly.

'I reckon we would,' Duffy augmented.

Banning said with less conviction: 'We hadn't ever done anything like that before.'

Shelby growled: 'Ain't none of us can remember how he felt that long ago. Except about them Munro men after they strung up the poor sonofabitch. Mad as hell about them.'

Banning shrugged his skinny shoulders. 'It certainly doesn't matter now, anyway. I recall we were not about to ride back into Munro right there and then. When they'd be expecting us to strike back at them for what they'd done. We were young, and crazy mad like Rich said: but we weren't that stupid. It surely did knock the stuffing out of us, losing a good friend that way. And it made us reckless and careless later. After the money from the Munro bank raid ran out.'

Miller said: 'Rich got that stiff leg of his from when he was shot and captured at a stage hold-up in Texas. Duff was caught, too.'

'Tried and found guilty,' Banning took up the account

again. 'Drew twenty-five years. And then Pete Race, Gene and me were caught when we tried to break them out of the wagon taking them to state prison. Tried and convicted and given the same twenty-five year sentences.

'So we were well past forty when we got out: nearly fifty a couple of us. Me one legged from when a wound turned gangrenous. Rich with his game leg. Gene near blind as a bat without his eyeglasses, Pete and Duff showing plenty of signs of old age before their time. A Texas prison and the hard labour they put us to, that does not make for growing old gracefully, let me tell you, Mr Edge.'

He was sheepishly ashamed for stretched seconds, needed two attempts to meet and hold Edge's incurious gaze, then admit: 'What I told you about us being in the army? Me a major? And Gene hunting buffalo? Pete whalin'...

'Wasn't true, none of it,' Miller said flatly.

'Except I done some bartendin',' Shelby put in sourly. 'And Duff got to be a pretty damn good teamster before he settled to the grocery trade.'

Duffy added morosely: 'It was stuff we dreamed up to cover what we'd been doing for all them years we were locked up in that Texas state prison. For the people here in Pomona.'

'Stuff we'd like to have done,' Shelby muttered.

Miller held his cup in both hands, squeezing hard like he was intent upon crushing it. He said bitterly: 'And the hell of it is, we didn't have no need to pull that stage hold-up outside of San Antone.'

'Nor that first Munro bank raid all them years ago,' Duffy added in the same tone of deep regret.

'That's right,' Banning agreed. 'We were young and wild in those days. But we had plans, and we made provision for them. A high proportion of the money and valuables we stole in the early years we cached in a safe place: for the future.'

'Some future,' Shelby growled. He made to spit at the stove, but swallowed the saliva with a scowl when he caught the reproachful glare from Duffy.

'When we were released from jail,' Banning continued the story, 'we headed straight for our hiding place. Divided up the spoils. It wasn't a fortune when it was split five ways, but it was enough. And we had no stomach for taking up the old life again.

'Pete Race had a brother and sister-in-law living here in Pomona, and we all drifted to this neck of the woods. Was a fine town in those days. People hoped for a prosperous future if the stage company routed their line through here.

'Pete, he went into partnership with his brother at the meat market. Duff operated a freight business, few years later opened this store. Rich met and married the widow of the man who had the bakery and they changed the name over the door. Gene bought the saloon, then the dry goods store. Me, I married, had a son who took over running the livery when my wife died and I'd had enough.

'We settled down real well, for desperadoes. Enjoyed the quiet life with our ill-gotten gains put to pretty good use. Not the high life we planned back when we were young and crazy wild. But . . .'

He shrugged. 'Just every now and then, after we heard the stage line was to be routed through Munro on the north trail, we talked about the people of that town. Now, in a way, the double double cross they pulled made us miss out on twenty five years of good life, good food in our bellies, fine liquor, young women . . .'

Duffy cut in: 'But we never done nothin' about it until the old schoolhouse burnt down. Then we told folks hereabouts that maybe we could raise the cash to build a new one. If they'd name it after an old buddy of ours.'

Banning said: 'Well, like you can see, Edge the people of Pomona don't take over-much pride in their community. Something of a dying town, I suppose, ever since the stage company chose the northern route.

'They were happy to agree to anything, long as they didn't have to get up off their butts and do any hard work. Or dig into their pockets for cash.

'I think, perhaps, we hoped that if we were able to give Pomona some civic pride, folks would start to take better care of what was their own.'

His expression showed, he held out little hope this would ever be so. 'It was going to be one final criminal act in our lives. We're old, dying in a decaying town. It seemed like a fine idea. To take our revenge for the lynching of Charlie Riley nearly fifty years ago, use the money for something worthwhile. Guess you know what I'm getting, at Edge?'

'I guess,' Edge replied on a trickle of cigarette smoke.

'I'm convinced you did stumble upon us in just the way you said. But perhaps it doesn't matter how it happened. You found us: a man who knows what we did at Munro. How we robbed the bank and the young deputy got killed. I'm hoping you're the kind of man who won't be too troubled by other folks' bad business. Long as you're not a loser?'

Edge wondered if Banning and the others truly did not know Nick Cornwall was just one of four people who were dead because of the old score that had been settled.

He shifted in his chair, to get more comfortable in the hard-seated ladderback.

But Rick Shelby, ever ready to be provoked, misconstrued the movement. His cup crashed to the floor, shattered, sprayed liquor-laced coffee across the clean surface.

In turn, Edge fleetingly misinterpreted this as an accident. And before he realised his mistake, Shelby had not realised his. Had jerked a Colt from under his dungarees, aimed it at Edge, thumb cocking the hammer.

'Aw no!' Banning groaned when, having seen Edge was covered, Duffy and Miller pulled their revolvers, dropped their cups to break on the floor. 'Mistake?'

Edge muttered through gritted teeth and pursed lips: 'I wasn't sure if I had an ax to grind here, feller. But I have so few rules I live by, I got to be ready to die for one of them.'

18

It was no idle boast that Edge was ready to die: he had always been prepared for sudden, violent death since the War Between the States started him out on the killing trails. Maybe before this, even: when he and his family worked the small farm in Iowa and the Sioux were an ever-present threat to peace and life.

And not for the first time he recognised it would be a futile way to end his life: once more he was risking his skin for no good reason.

But then...

The grocery was one of those Pomona stores with boarding on the street out front. And the setting down of a booted foot on warped and weathered timber distracted everyone: including Edge.

Then a familiar cultured voice said: 'Those are my feelings precisely, Mr Edge.'

The half-breed had a fleeting glimpse of an auburn-haired city-suited figure in the doorway, silhouetted against the sun-bright street. And immediately abandoned his intended lunge upright: rose slowly and did not reach for his holstered Colt. Instead made as if to push up both hands in the time-honoured gesture of surrender.

The four old-timers all peered at the doorway now. And as they recognised the Philadelphia schoolteacher, for a vital moment they were unaware that Edge surged out of slow motion. Brought up his right leg, smashed the underside of the booted foot against the top of the stove: uprooted it from the floor and wrenched the smokestack out of its seating at the back.

At that moment Conrad Christie triggered a shot from the Winchester levelled at his hip, and the bullet ricocheted off the metal of the canted-over stove as it belched smoke and spilled flaring cordwood.

The guns of Shelby, Miller and Duffy swung toward the doorway a part second after their shocked gazes became transfixed there. Then all three jerked upright so violently their chairs crashed over.

Banning was slower, struggling frantically to get to his feet with the leverage of the stick as he clawed desperately for the gun inside his dungarees.

Just for a moment, perhaps, before the billowing black smoke veiled the scene, the frightened one-legged leader of the one-time bunch of desperadoes glimpsed the flash of a silvered blade as Edge's hand swung from out of the long hair at the nape of his neck: fisted around the handle of the straight razor he carried in a pouch held at the top of his spine by a beaded leather thong.

Then a deafeningly loud fusillade of gunfire exploded within the confines of the store that no longer smelled good: chokingly filled with the fumes of burning wood, hot metal, black powder smoke and fear. As Edge, wary of being hit by a wildly-fired bullet from the rifle in Christie's inexpert hands ducked down behind a man.

Employed the shaving tool as a weapon. Thrust forward and up with the hand that gripped it, moved it in a backward stabbing action, dragged it down, withdrew it toward himself.

Heard the piercingly shrill scream of Rich Shelby as the man endured the shock, then the fear, next the pain of the awesome wound. A gaping fissure in his flesh that began at the navel, ran down to the base of his belly, through his genitals until the honed blade was jerked out from between his legs by a hand sodden with warm blood.

Still in a crouch, Edge lunged to the side. Hurled himself over and down behind the length of counter that ran across the rear of the store, banged into the wall of shelves in back, covered his head with his arms against the battering of jars, sacks, bottles and cans that rained down on him.

He didn't have time to wipe Shelby's life blood off the blade of the razor before he closed it into the handle, stowed it back into the neck pouch. Nor to be concerned about the crimson slipperiness of his hand as he drew the Frontier Colt and the front of the counter where he crouched was pitted by bullets.

The store was filled with clamorous sound. Men were shouting. Shelby was still screaming. Flames began to roar as the spewed-out contents of the overturned stove found fresh fuel to feed upon. He recognised the deeper cracks of the more powerful Winchester still firing against the crackle of handguns. The noises he made when he scampered over the supplies littered floor behind the rear counter, then around the angle and along the side wall were totally blanketed.

He knew he had played some high risk percentages: for a start had certainly never counted on Christie showing up when he did. Knew if the Philadelphia schoolteacher had not done so, he would probably be dead on the grocery floor by now.

He was alive, but if he took any more long-odds chances, he might not stay that way. He straightened up, levelled the Colt from his hip, swung it from right to left through a fast, short arc, squeezed the trigger, fanned the hammer with the heel of his left hand. Fired blind into the rolling turbulance of the smoke. Pumped off three shots. Then turned. Ran toward the front of the store.

Had an image of the sun-bright display window shining like heaven's entrance through the smoke that could have come from the fires of hell.

He ducked his head low, pushed a shoulder forward, took a powerful leap and sailed through and over the displays of groceries. Shattered the window glass into a million glittering shards.

In mid-flight he smelled the cold, fresh air. And it made him feel drunkenly elated to be clear of the noxious atmosphere within the store.

The momentum of the leap was used up and he arced down, smacked against the hard-packed street. He was ready for the force of impact: had folded his body into a tight ball to absorb the jolt in non-vital areas. But they were nonetheless susceptible to pain and the crunching landing hurt.

Not enough, though, to close his mind to the danger that still existed. And he was able to suppress the compelling need

157

to lay down and rest. Hauled himself to his feet, unsteadily balanced on splayed legs, gun levelled in his hand.

His vision cleared when he shook his head and he looked to left and right. Saw his horse had jerked free of the hitching post and now stood, shuddering with equine fear of fire, halfway up the sharply curved street to the right. The less pronounced bend to the left was deserted. But there was a group of fast-moving riders out on the trail, still about a mile beyond the eastern town limits marker.

The city-suited man remained at the doorway of the grocery store: unmindful of the smoke that billowed out. Contributed to it as he methodically levered the action and squeezed the trigger of the Winchester, blasting shots into the store until the magazine was empty. Kept up the same series of movement after the rifle ceased to buck with recoil.

Would certainly have died as he went on uselessly levering the action and squeezing the trigger of the empty rifle had Edge not made it to the doorway in a staggering run, used a painfully bruised shoulder to barge the schoolteacher aside.

A moment before a hail of gunfire exploded out through the smoke filled doorway. Then one, another and a third form came over the threshold. Each with a smoke-sooted face, body run with blood. They staggered to the centre of the street, banging into each other, trying to fire their empty guns as they raked them from side to side.

Duffy, Miller, Banning. Unable to hold out any longer against the demands of their bullet-riddled bodies now they were clear of the choking smoke and raging heat. And one by one, coincidentally in order of seniority within their group, they pitched to the ground.

Duffy and Miller dead before they lay still. Banning able to support himself for a few final moments on his cane as he moved his head, searched for and found the half-breed and the schoolteacher. Peered at both of them with a kind of reproachful sadness: this unlikely partnership of a Westerner and an Easterner that had caused the downfall of his bunch of one-time desperadoes.

When the one-legged man became inert in death, Christie slumped against the front wall of the burning building, held out the Winchester, said:

'It was Alice's rifle. You don't mind I used it to steal your thunder, Mr Edge?'

The half-breed told him: 'That what it was, feller? I had it down as a storm in a coffee-cup.'

People peered out of their houses and business premises toward the grocery store that soon would be as devasted by fire as the former school next door. A few stepped out on to both curves of the sloping street, but none advanced on the smoke-hung scene of carnage where three men lay dead, one appeared dazed to the point of exhaustion and another camly extracted spent cartridges from his revolver, pushed fresh rounds into the chambers.

'You followed me, feller?' Edge asked, slid the reloaded Colt into his holster, wiped his bloodied hand down a pants leg.

The wall Christie leaned against had grown hot and he stepped away from it. Almost dropped the rifle, but held on to it by the muzzle end, used the Winchester as a kind of crutch to help him stay on his feet as he moved beyond the range of the searing heat of the fire.

'Didn't you know?' He seemed indifferent about getting an answer.

'Not aboard the Conestoga?'

'No. Horseback. I left the mount outside of town.'

Edge suppressed the urge to cold anger. Showed a smile that caused his ice blue eyes to glint between their narrowed lids, exposed just a thin line of his teeth through drawn-back lips. Drawled evenly: 'Guess I was thinking more of what was ahead of me than behind. But I have to believe I'd have known about you if you'd meant me no good.'

Christie obviously failed to grasp the precise meaning of this. He waved a weary hand at the three corpses sprawled face down on the centre of the street, jerked his head toward the burning grocery store. 'Not you, Edge. Them. And I knew you were the kind of man who wouldn't give up until——'

'Wrong,' Edge cut in, struck a match on the jutting butt of his Colt in the holster, to relight the cigarette that had been angled from the side of his mouth ever since the start of the violence. 'When I left Munro, I figured Munro business was all behind me. It was California ahead of me so occupied my mind I didn't know you were trailing me.'

Christie's long face under the sandy hair expressed disbelief, next surprise, then resignation. Before he shrugged, said: 'You mean ... Well, the way it turned out, it was for the best?'

Edge looked out along the east trail, where the riders were drawing closer, no longer galloped their mounts in response to the gunfire. Their progress slowed as they saw the smoke of the fire, maybe recognised the two men who had survived the flying bullets and the flames. 'Harry Grimes have the same wrong idea about me?'

Christie looked eastwards, swaying, blinking, swallowing hard: suffering the first symptoms of delayed shock. He obviously became aware of the group of a half dozen riders for the first time.

'I don't think so. I understood when he found out what you told his wife in the saloon—about the first bank robbery and the lynching all those years ago—he telegraphed several local and federal law offices. With the names of the old men. He hoped, the kind of men they were, they would have been arrested. That prison records might show where they went eventually. I suppose he must have been lucky with his enquiries?'

Edge nodded, said: 'Maybe, feller.' He turned away from Christie. 'And maybe I'll see you in California.'

'No, not me, Mr Edge. I'm going back to Philadelphia. Perhaps my wife ... Or maybe not. But without Alice ...' He shrugged.

Edge went unhurriedly to where his now calmed horse waited.

A woman, standing back from the open doorway of her house, accused bitterly: 'They were old men! Crippled and long past their prime! They never had any chance against a man like you!'

The half-breed swung up into his saddle, answered: 'They were old desperadoes who just couldn't give up, lady. Never lost the Edge.'

160